ALSO BY STEVEN BUTLER

The Nothing to See Here Hotel Series

The Nothing to See Here Hotel

You Ain't Seen Nothing Yeti!

Sea-ing is Believing!

Fiend of the Seven Sewers

STEVEN BUTLER
ILLUSTRATED BY CLAIRE POWELL

SIMON & SCHUSTER

First published in Great Britain in 2022 by Simon & Schuster UK Ltd

Text copyright © 2022 Steven Butler
Illustrations copyright © 2022 Claire Powell

1 3 5 7 9 10 8 6 4 2

Simon & Schuster UK Ltd
1st Floor, 222 Gray's Inn Road
London
WC1X 8HB

www.simonandschuster.co.uk
www.simonandschuster.com.au
www.simonandschuster.co.in

Simon & Schuster Australia, Sydney
Simon & Schuster India, New Delhi

A CIP catalogue record for this book is available from the British Library.

PB ISBN 978-1-4711-9923-3
eBook ISBN 978-1-4711-9924-0
eAudio ISBN 978-1-4711-9928-8

Printed and bound by CPI Group (UK) Ltd, Croydon, CR0 4YY

MIX
Paper from
responsible sources
FSC
www.fsc.org FSC® C171272

For Jane Griffiths:
Editor of The Nothing to See Here Hotel
and inspiration for Ella Jane Griffin

CONTENTS

1

SO THIS IS HOME?

The town of Cod's Bottom was a miserable little place, squashed between the foot of steep cliffs and the spiteful sea. Its slate buildings were huddled together like squat grey piglets jostling for space at feeding time, and everything was covered in layer upon layer of seagull poo.

Ella Griffin looked out from the front step of her new home and grimaced.

'I wonder how long it would take for *us* to get covered in bird droppings like that?' she thought out loud. 'Not long, I bet.'

'Stop it, darling,' said Mum from the open front door, fumbling with her coat.

'Ten minutes and I'll be splattered in the stuff. *Splish! Splash! Sploo!* The princess of—'

'I'm not listening . . .' Mum stepped out into the chilly

1

evening air, closing the door behind
her, as Wilson, the family's French bulldog, snuffled at
Ella's heels. 'Isn't this a lovely place? The rain's stopped
for us, look!'

Ella glanced along her new street, Cuttlebone
Lane, and eyed the fishermen's cottages on either side,
as wonky and worn as a set of rotten teeth. She tried
desperately to spot anything even remotely lovely about
the town that squeezed in around her, but failed.

'I . . . I don't know,'
Ella replied as a sad,
empty feeling swooshed
through her body and
pooled in her blue
wellington boots,
squelching between
her toes.

How could this
be their home?
It was so much
worse than
Ella ever
imagined.
Was Mum
secretly
punishing

her for hiding snacks under her bed, or for that time she'd tried to climb the bedroom curtains and accidentally ripped them off the wall?

'I had a brilliant childhood here,' Mum cooed happily. She gave Wilson's lead a little tug and set off down the hill towards the harbour.

'I was having a brilliant childhood too, in London,' Ella called as Mum and Wilson continued walking away. She knew she was pushing her luck, but Ella couldn't help herself. 'London isn't covered in giant splats of—'

'Yes, all right,' Mum snapped over her shoulder. She stopped in her tracks and shot Ella one of her 'You're not too old to be sent to your room!' stares. 'I get it! But you'll soon love Cod's Bottom, I promise. Let's go look at the sea and breathe some fresh air before the sun sets. It's good for you.'

'I can't!' Ella gasped in mock horror. She skittered across the wet pavement, trying not to slip as she caught up to Mum and Wilson.

'Why not?'

Ella took a deep sniff of the air, then pretended to be sick into her gloved hands. She was relieved to see Mum give a tiny smirk. 'This place smells just like its name – FISH BUM!'

'It's Cod's Bottom!'

'Wilson thinks so, don't you, boy?' Ella joked, making

the roly-poly pooch bark and wriggle about. 'See? Wilsy thinks it smells of fish bum too!'

Mum raised an eyebrow and tried very hard to look cross, even though she was stifling a laugh.

'You've made your point . . . Look, I know this was all a tiny bit quick.'

Ella said nothing, ignoring the urge to cry that bubbled in the back of her mind. *Quick?* Mum packed up their old flat so fast she nearly broke the sound barrier! Even worse, this was only the beginning of the summer holidays. Ella had weeks before she could distract herself from all this gloom with some brain-boggling schoolwork.

'I know you miss London. I do as well . . . but things will be great here, you'll see.' Mum put an arm round Ella's shoulder and pulled her into a hug. 'London didn't have this wonderful view, did it?'

Ella's eyes darted to the narrow sliver of sea visible at the end of Cuttlebone Lane. They had only been in Cod's Bottom for two days, but she was already certain she might die of boredom pretty soon. Where was the noise and traffic? The interesting people and Alfie's Burger Bar? Her Saturday drama club? Boredom was going to get her for sure. Ella could just *feel* it. Any day now, Mum would come in to wake her and find a dried up, girl-shaped husk in her bed. A shrivelled boredom-mummy in panda pyjamas!

She glanced back at their new home, Minerva Mansions, perched at the top of the lane like a lopsided wedding cake gone soggy in the rain. From Mum's curly-cornered photographs, Ella knew the block of apartments had once been painted a smart, forget-me-not blue, with flower boxes on every window ledge. Now, years of damp and grime had turned it the colour of an old bruise and it seemed to have slumped lazily against the building next door. If homes could talk, this one would probably be groaning *Oh, my aching bones!*

'Come on,' Mum said, starting off with Wilson again. 'We can't dawdle for too long. There are suitcases to unpack, plus I promised Miss Jenkins I'd pick up some groceries for her.'

'Which neighbour is Miss Jenkins?' asked Ella, hurrying to catch up. 'The upstairs lady who shouts at the telly, or the downstairs lady with weird smells coming from under her door?'

'I'm warning you!' Mum's hard stare powered up into one of her mega glares.

'I just wondered.'

'You mustn't make jokes about people.'

'I wasn't,' Ella said, holding up her palms like she was surrendering after a crime.

'Well, if you must know, Miss Jenkins lives in the flat upstairs. How did you know she shouts at the television?'

'I heard her last night,' Ella mumbled. 'She was hollering about something on the news. A proper strop-wobbler!'

Mum snickered for only a nanosecond, but Ella spotted it and felt herself relax. She pulled out her treasured green notebook and matching green pen from her coat pocket, turned to a list she'd already started under the heading Cod's Bottomers, and scribbled Miss Jenkins's name next to where it already said

Upstairs lady - bit scary. Proper grannysaurus. Shouts at the telly.

Mum sighed as they trudged downhill. 'I know it's strange,' she said. 'Sometimes life throws these things at us. No one was expecting your poor Aunt Sylvie to . . . to . . . um—'

'Die.' Ella finished Mum's sentence. She already knew what the word meant.

'Yep, that,' Mum continued. 'And now her home belongs to me . . . to us. It's where Sylvie and I grew up together. We moved here when I was just your age. I was worried at first, too. But you'll love living in Cod's Bottom, just like I did.'

Ella nodded.

'Think of this as a new adventure,' Mum said with a sad smile.

Ella smiled back, ignoring the shiver that ran down her spine. What kind of adventure was this!?

At the bottom of the lane the cobbles opened onto the promenade, which crept around the edge of the dreary harbour.

'Ta-dah!' said Mum with a smile. 'Do you want to entertain yourself here or come grocery shopping with me?'

'I thought we were off to have an adventure,' Ella reminded her. What on earth was she supposed to do on her own? Count the seagull poos on the post office roof? An image of herself as the SHRIVELLED BOREDOM-MUMMY flashed across her mind again.

'We *will*, darling,' Mum said, handing her Wilson's lead. 'But someone has to do the chores first. So, what'll it be?'

'We'll stay out here,' mumbled Ella, admitting defeat.

'Good girl,' Mum said. 'Keep out of trouble, the pair of you, and I'll meet you back here in a jiffy. I'll be as quick as I can.' With that, Mum smoothed Ella's curly red hair, planted a kiss on her forehead, and hurried into the Laughing Starfish Store, letting the door swing shut behind her with a loud *TING-A-LING-A-LING!*

'Okey-dokey,' Ella mumbled, setting off along the harbour wall with Wilson huffing behind her. 'No one likes a Mopey Mildred, do they? Come on, Wilsy – let's go and find some fun.'

They'd barely gone more than a few steps before Ella's thoughts wandered to her best friends, Ava and Yusif. 'What are those beasties up to back in London, eh, Wilson? I bet they've been rehearsing lines for theatre club all day,' Ella mused as she realised it was Saturday. 'And laughing loads and loads without me.' She'd been planning to audition for the part of Juliet this term and had even figured out how to plant a kiss on Romeo's slobber-chopsy boy-germ cheek without being sick and everything. She'd practised on Wilson's stubby snout. Then Mum announced they were moving to Fish Bum and her chances were snuffed out. *KA-POW!* Whatever Ava and Yusif were up to, Ella was pretty sure it would be more exciting than sightseeing along the promenade. She'd give them a call before bed and find out.

Down the road a little, Ella spotted people coming and going. She tried smiling to a few of the friendlier-looking ones, but nobody smiled back. Everybody seemed just as glum as she was feeling. The whole town was one big globule of gloom. THIS PLACE WAS GLOOMSVILLE!

'They're all so warm and chatty, aren't they?' Ella joked to Wilson, but the snorty French bulldog just yanked his lead in the direction of a seagull perched on a bin overflowing with greasy chip-shop paper.

'WILL *YOU* BE MY FRIEND?' Ella yelled at the startled bird. It shrieked and whirled off into the air, wings and legs flailing, making Wilson bark excitedly. They both watched it fly out to sea, a tiny bright dot against the glowering sky.

Ella sighed to herself. Now what? Maybe she could do tiny pigeon-steps all the way from one end of the seafront to the other and count them as she went? Or . . . she could make a fishing rod out of a stick and try to catch a shark from the rocks? Maybe not . . .

Maybe she *would* go and explore . . . Mum had told her to think of their new town as an adventure, after all.

The rickety pier and its lopsided lighthouse were closed due to the bad weather, so Ella headed off along the harbour wall instead, dragging a reluctant Wilson behind her and enjoying the jellied smack of her wellingtons against the wet cobbles.

'This calls for a list, Wilsy,' Ella said, pulling out her green notebook again.

Ella loved making lists. Mum always joked that it was her 'superpower'. Ella had been jotting things down ever since she first learned to read and write. Right now, there was a box in her new bedroom crammed with stacks of old notebooks all jam-packed with lists. Lists made the world seem safe when Ella was nervous and it felt good to know everything she'd ever seen, heard, tried, touched, thought, found or tasted was neatly arranged in rows on crisp white pages, and that she could look at them again any time she liked.

'We don't want to miss anything, do we?' She turned to a new page and wrote Things in Cod's Bottom across the top. Then, with a giggle, Ella scribbled it out and wrote Things in Fish Bum instead.

'Right. Let's start from here.' She looked both ways, then, feeling more comforted already, started to write.

Pier — closed (BORING!)
The Laughing Starfish Store
The post office (a lot more bird
   poo than the other shops?)
A boy kicking a ball
Two seagulls fighting for leftover
   chips
Mrs Markham's wool shop
   (s—n—o—o—z—e!)
The fishmonger's (MEGA WHIFFY)
A crate of sardines
A lady with a screaming baby
The Crab and Conch Shell pub
A rusty bike with a missing front
   wheel

A tall man with a clipboard
The fishermen's yard (EVEN MORE
  MEGA WHIFFY!!!)
A boat named Barnacle Betty
A dog barking at a cat
A cat hissing at a dog

Ella looked up from her list and frowned. There, at the far end of the promenade was a strangely shaped building she hadn't noticed before. This was only the second time she'd been down to the waterfront, and the first time she'd ventured so far along the seawall.

'What do you think it is, Wilsy?' Ella asked the portly dog, but he was too preoccupied with sniffing at lampposts to even glance her way.

She hurried him past a newsagent's, not bothering to add it to her list, and as they got closer, Ella could see there were large metal gates in front of the building, a chain and padlock twisted through them. On either side, crumbling statues of angels in long, drapey dresses wept streaks of seagull poo down their pale cheeks.

'Ooh! Only exciting places are kept behind gates with chains and padlocks!' she told Wilson as she peered through the metal bars. Her eyes widened and she drew in a gasp of chilly air.

Beyond the rusted gates was a huge derelict building

that stood half on a jut of rock at the base of the cliff and half on rotting wooden stilts over the foaming breakers. Ella couldn't believe her eyes. It looked like a museum or evil scientist's lair or . . . something she couldn't put her finger on. She searched around for clues, trying to figure out what the old place might be.

Before her, a path led from the gate to an wide ornate entranceway with red and gold doors, topped with a stained-glass dome. Most of the glass was smashed or had fallen away, and the painted wood was peeling and cracked. A high archway above the entrance was carved with dozens of plump cherubs, each holding a musical instrument, and their faces were all turned towards the gates, as if they were expecting someone to arrive.

All the hairs on the back of Ella's neck stood up on end as she met the cherubs' lifeless gaze. 'Good afternoon,' she whispered to them, trying not to laugh at their naked bottoms. 'Were you waiting for me?'

The cherubs didn't reply . . .

Above the gaggle of plump stone babies stretched row upon row of broken windows like open mouths showing jagged fangs. The wind howled through them and made the building seem as if it was groaning in the cold; scraps of tatty curtains flapped in and out like tongues.

'This place is amazing!' Ella hooted down at Wilson,

but he wasn't impressed, too busy sniffing at something small and white on the ground instead. 'What have you got there, boy?'

Ella bent down, picked up the object and examined it. There, sitting in her green-gloved palm, was a podgy-fingered stone hand. It must have come from one of the cherubs.

'Anybody lose some dinky digits?' she called up to the statues above the doors. 'No? Oh, well . . .'

Ella scanned the building higher still, spotting that the roof was a mass of crumbling domes and turrets surrounded by stone angels, like the ones on either side of the gates.

'What *is* this place?' She turned to a new page in her trusty notebook and wrote Adventure Building across the top. Glancing this way and that, Ella tried to decide which details to write down first, when she noticed something.

Above the stained-glass dome, it was possible to make out the words COD'S BOTTOM HIPPODROME: PALACE OF VARIETIES in faded letters across the brickwork.

'It's a THEATRE!' Ella yelped as her heart leaped into her throat with excitement. Why hadn't Mum told her about *this*? She'd wanted to be an actor ever since she was old enough to walk and talk! Maybe Cod's Bottom had a Saturday drama club like the one back in London!

'I might not turn into a shrivelled boredom-mummy after all, Wilsy!'

Ella started to frantically write in her notebook.

Eight doors
A squillion cherubs
Crumbly angels
Smashed stained-glass dome
A girl at the window

Hang on . . . a GIRL AT THE—?

Standing at one of the top-floor windows was a pale young woman with blonde hair scraped back in a bun. She was strangely delicate and elfin, dressed in what looked like a white ballerina's tutu.

A ballerina! Maybe they teach dance lessons at this theatre!

'If they teach dance lessons,' Ella whispered to Wilson, ignoring how terrifically closed-down the old place looked, 'I bet they teach acting classes here as well . . .'

She tucked her notebook under her arm and waved.

'HELLO! LOOK DOWN HERE!'

The girl didn't react. She just stared blankly into the distance.

'Hey! Can you let me in? The gates are locked.' Ella waved again, and was just about to shout a third time, when . . .

'There you are!' A hand planted itself firmly on

her shoulder. 'I couldn't find you.'

Ella almost jumped out of her raincoat as she screamed and spun round, dropping her notebook into a puddle with a dull *SPLOSH!*

'What are you doing, darling?' It was Mum. She had brown paper grocery bags tucked under each arm and an impatient expression on her face. 'Time to get home. The weather's on the turn.'

'You scared me!' Ella blurted. She glanced over Mum's shoulder and realised it was getting dark. How had she not noticed it had also started to rain? Retrieving her notebook from the puddle, she wiped it on her coat sleeve and shoved it back into her pocket.

'I've been calling from the other end of the promenade. Trust you two not to be listening! I thought dogs were meant to have good hearing!'

'Sorry, I was looking at—'

'The theatre?' Mum interrupted. 'I know. I didn't think it would be long before you found it.'

'Why didn't you tell me?' Ella said, gesturing wildly above her head for extra dramatic effect. 'This changes everything! I need to find out about classes.'

Mum rolled her eyes and turned to go. 'Don't be ridiculous.'

'What?' Ella replied. 'I'm not! I want to do acting classes here.'

'Nonsense,' said Mum. 'Look at it, Ella – it's been closed since before *I* was your age. The council are knocking it down soon, so they definitely don't teach classes in there. The place is a death trap. Honestly!'

'Yes they do!' Ella turned back to the theatre and peered up at the top-floor window. 'SEE! Oh . . .'

The girl was gone. Only a scrap of old curtain fluttered silently where she'd been standing moments before.

'But I saw—'

'Come on, you two,' Mum said firmly as she started hurrying back along the seafront. 'Let's get home quick – it's getting late and a storm is rolling in.'

Ella hesitated, still staring up at the window. Hadn't there just been . . . ? Goosebumps prickled across her skin and a shudder crept up her spine.

'Let's go, Wilson,' she muttered as thunder rumbled overhead, and, for reasons she couldn't quite fathom, Ella suddenly felt the need to get away from the Cod's Bottom Hippodrome as fast as she could.

Cod Bottomers List.

2
A RESTLESS NIGHT

'Oh, my goodness!' A woman stood at the entrance of Minerva Mansions, waving her arms at the two figures who stumbled along Cuttlebone Lane. 'Run fer it, dears!'

Mum and Ella had only left the theatre a short while ago, but already heavy rain was lashing the fishermen's cottages in great horizontal sheets. The wind had blown up so ferociously Ella thought she might suddenly be swept away as she wobbled homewards with Wilson held tightly to her chest.

'Hurry, darling!' Mum spluttered over her shoulder. She was soaked through and her paper shopping bags had started to fall apart, leaving a trail of jam jars and soup tins behind her on the pavement. 'KEEP GOING!'

'We're right behind you,' Ella yelled, jumping over groceries, but the wind snatched her words away and flung them up and over the rooftops. She squinted against the downpour and sprinted as fast as she could towards the warm glow spilling from the open door of their new . . . *home*. Ella winced as the word crossed her mind.

'There you are, dears!' The scrawny lady on the doorstep cheered as Mum and Ella approached. 'I thought we'd lost you!' She hopped aside as the two bedraggled humans and their very bedraggled dog finally rocketed indoors and tumbled onto the hallway rug in a sopping wet heap. 'Worried sick, I was! Haven't seen a sea squall like this one in months, and I noticed you both popping out earlier. Storms come out of nowhere in these parts, y'see – even in summer. Surprised you'd forgotten, Mrs Griffin.'

Mum, who was lying face down among the last surviving groceries and scraps of paper bag, grunted into the floor. She turned her face sideways. 'Ella, this is Mrs Clott . . . our downstairs neighbour.'

Ella glanced up, bleary-eyed, at the silhouetted figure standing over her. So this was the person with strange smells coming from her flat. She'd have to write that in the trusty notebook later.

'Never go out when a sea squall's on the horizon, dears,' Mrs Clott continued, picking something off her gums with a chewed fingernail. She seemed far more interested in chatting than helping Ella or Mum get up

19

off the floor. 'You're asking for trouble if you do. That's what my dadsy always said, he did. My great-nana was clean blown away in a Cod's Bottom squall once, don't you know. *Poof!* They found her three weeks later in *France*, dazed and confused!'

Ella wriggled to her feet and Mrs Clott fixed her with a crooked smile. She didn't expect Ella to believe what she'd said, surely?

The woman chuckled. 'You're officially a Cod's Bottomer now, little lady,' and she shoved the front door closed against the wind. 'A proper Cod's Bottom belle!'

Ella wasn't too sure she was happy to hear that, but she didn't want to be rude to her new neighbour so she nodded through the strands of soaked hair that clung to her face.

'I feel more like a yeti than a Cod's Bottom belle!' Ella joked, before extending her hand for Mrs Clott to shake it. 'I'm Ella Griffin. It's nice to meet you properly.'

'Tabitha Clott,' Mrs Clott replied, ignoring Ella's outstretched hand. 'Have you enjoyed your first few days at Minerva Mansions, Elsie?

Ella rubbed her side where she'd landed on a tin of sliced

peaches and examined Mrs Clott while she tried to think of a polite answer.

Tabitha was an odd spectacle indeed – so tall and thin she could have been a skeleton standing there in the hallway (if skeletons wore flowery aprons and had their hair in rollers). Her lipstick-smeared mouth cracked into a smile again, exposing a set of teeth the colour of mouldy cheese. Yellow surrounded by pink . . . like a pimple ready to be popped.

'Mmm-hmm,' Ella finally replied. She breathed in – and instantly regretted it. There was that strange smell again. It was the horrible zing of nose-stingingly sour perfume combined with the funk of floor polish and boiled sweets. It surrounded Mrs Clott like her very own pollution cloud. 'It's . . . erm . . . lovely to be here.'

'Well, don't be lounging around in the hall when you're both soaking wet, ladies,' Tabitha said with a shrug and another pimple-coloured grin. 'You'll catch your deaths . . . and you're leaving a puddle on the floor there, Elsie.'

'It's Ella,' Ella mumbled, but Tabitha wasn't listening. 'I'm *Ella* Griffin.'

'I'll not be mopping up after you girlies, mind,' the bony woman half said, half coughed. 'It's ever so good to see you both, but we mop up our own puddles at Minerva Mansions.' With that, as if anxious to avoid helping them further, Mrs Clott turned and hurried back towards her smelly flat at the foot of the stairs. At the door she turned and added, 'Do pop by for a cuppa sometimes though, won't you?'

Mum opened her mouth to reply, but Tabitha wasn't waiting for an answer. 'Bye, Mrs Griffin . . . and Elsie,' she croaked as she closed her door, leaving Mum and Ella alone and dripping in the silence of the hallway . . . well . . . sort of silence.

With their downstairs neighbour gone, Ella's mind instantly turned to her lists. She slipped her hand into her pocket to make sure she hadn't lost the little notebook in the storm, then tilted her head to listen, wondering what noises were worth writing down. Mum knew exactly what Ella was doing and smiled, letting her daughter have a second to take it all in.

As Ella's ears adjusted, it felt like Minerva Mansions was quietly nattering to itself: the wind and rain hammering on the hall window, Mrs Clott's radio burbling, a toilet flushing, Wilson snorting, a clock ticking, seabirds crying in the storm, the walls creaking, a tap dripping, and footsteps padding along a corridor somewhere upstairs all combined to make a low rumble that filled the air with an odd, restless quality. A not-quite-silence.

'All done?' Mum asked after a moment.

'All done,' Ella said with a nod, trying to shake off the feeling of uneasiness.

'Right.' Mum bent down to retrieve what was left of the paper shopping bags. 'Let's get the kettle on and warm ourselves a bit.'

Letting Wilson snuffle and grunt along ahead, they made their way up the stairs to their new home on the first floor.

'I fancy a baked potato,' Mum muttered to herself, as she reached the door and fumbled for the keys in her pocket, 'with cheese and beans . . . and a great big mug of steaming hot—'

'AAAAARGH!'

Before Mum could even finish her sentence, an ear-shattering screech erupted from the flat above.

'Oh, bum!' Mum whispered, pulling a face at Ella.

She grimaced and mouthed, '*I forgot to take Miss Jenkins her groceries.*' Her eyes darted towards the ceiling. 'She's yelling at the telly again.'

Ella didn't say anything. She didn't have to.

'Everyone here is very nice,' Mum whispered, knowing exactly what Ella was thinking. 'I promise.' Then, with one last groan, she handed Ella the door keys and trudged up the next flight of steps with their noisy neighbour's soggy groceries.

'Wish me luck,' she whimpered over her shoulder. 'If I'm not back in five minutes, call the police.'

Ella waited until Mum had vanished round the bend in the stairs before jabbing the key in the lock and heading inside. She kicked off her wellington boots behind the front door and padded across the hall into the kitchen. She'd just had time to fill up Wilson's water bowl when the shouting started again upstairs.

'WHERE'S THE REST OF IT, GRIFFIN?' Miss Jenkins's voice screamed. 'THIS ISN'T EVERY-THING I ASKED FOR!'

'I'm so sorry, Evelyn,' Mum's voice pleaded from above. 'I dropped a few things in the storm.'

'MY CUSTARD CREAMS?' Miss Jenkins howled. 'MY MUSHY PEAS? GET OUT OF MY SIGHT!'

Ella couldn't help giggling as she listened. 'Come on then, Wilsy,' she said when she'd heard enough squawking from upstairs. 'Let's go and do something fun while we wait for Mum.'

Marching back into the hall, Ella headed past the toilet and the living room and on to the door right at the end. Although she wouldn't admit it to Mum just yet, there was ONE GOOD THING about their shabby new home – HER BEDROOM! It used to be Mum and Sylvie's room when they were kids, and it was HUGE compared to her old room in London. Ella secretly LOVED it! She stopped and smiled at the ELLA'S ROOM sign that Mum had helped her nail to the door. Ava and Yusif had bought it for her as a going-away present.

'Miss you, beasties,' Ella said, tracing a finger along the curly letters of her name. She allowed herself a moment to sigh as lightning flashed at the windows and more thunder rumbled overhead, then Ella shrugged the sad feeling away, opened the door and headed inside.

'Here, we are, Wilsy –' Ella let the little dog run ahead of her – 'our new HQ!'

Mum had made sure the boxes of Ella's belongings were the first things off the removal van when they'd arrived two days ago, and Ella had spent most of the time since getting her room just how she wanted it.

Ella's favourite planets-of-the-solar-system mobile hung over her new bed, and a framed picture of Frida

Kahlo had pride of place on the wall behind it. Her enormous collection of books, comics and plays (there were 274 the last time Ella counted) had already been sorted by colour, and they looked brilliant on the shelves that stood on both sides of the door. The calavera skull lamp that Aunt Sylvie had brought back from a holiday in Mexico sat on the desk next to the window, and strings of fairy lights zigzagged across the ceiling.

No one could deny the room looked terrific. To Ella, it was PERFECT!

'I think we'd better make ourselves comfy,' Ella said to Wilson, who had already jumped onto the bed and was plodding round in little circles to find just the right snoozing spot. 'Mum's going to be a while, calming down the grannysaurus.'

Ella pulled off her damp scarf and gloves and draped them over the back of the chair, then she started unbuttoning her coat. 'I feel like we've been through a car wash without a car! I hope my lists aren't all wrinkled.'

She hung her coat on the back of the door, then fished inside its pockets to retrieve the green notepad and pen. Ella's fingers had just closed round the edge of the slightly soggy notebook when—

'What's this?' Her thumb had grazed against something cold and hard. She plucked the little object out from the folds of her coat and saw it was the stone hand she'd found by the theatre gates. She'd completely forgotten about it.

A tingle of . . . what was it exactly? Excitement? Nervousness? Whatever it was, it crept up her arms and made the hairs on the back of her neck bristle.

'Someone will be missing you,' Ella said, turning the peculiar little object over to examine it again. 'No one can play a harp with only one hand.'

The thought of all those cherubs staring lifelessly at the theatre gates made Ella shudder. The poor things were out there right now in this terrible weather, being lashed by the rain. She imagined them shifting their gaze to glare across the bay at Minerva Mansions, and her skin tingled with goosebumps. Ella delicately placed the tiny hand next to her framed photograph of Aunt Sylvie on the bookshelves by her bedroom door, then headed across the room to the tall window.

'I wonder if we can see the theatre from here, Wilsy?' Wilson snorted and rolled onto his back, burying his head under the pillow. 'Not in the mood, eh?' she said.

Ella tried to peer out into the stormy evening. 'It gets dark so early around here . . .' With all the lights on, the only thing Ella could see was the reflection of her own bedroom, a snoring dog on the bed and a red-haired girl who looked just like her staring straight back.

'Get out of my way!' Ella snapped at herself in the

glass. 'I can't see the theatre with you standing there!'

She quickly darted about, unplugging all the strings of fairy lights and switching off the skull lamp, then she returned to the window. Instantly, the outside world came into view and Ella squashed her face against the glass to get a better look across the lopsided houses of Cod's Bottom. From Minerva Mansions' vantage point at the top end of Cuttlebone Lane, the view was a lot better than she'd expected. It had been too foggy to see anything for the past two days, but the sea squall had finally blown the mists away. Even storms had their uses . . .

'Where are you?' Ella murmured, steaming up the windowpane. 'Show . . .'

Lightning sliced the sky in two and she could suddenly make out the forest of chimneypots that sloped down towards the harbour below. In the rickety lighthouse's rotating beam and the glow of the streetlamps that lined the promenade, Ella saw waves thundering up against the fishermen's yard, practically swallowing the pier whole. It was a miracle the entire town hadn't been washed away years ago.

'Where's the theatre?' Ella's eyes followed the harbour wall, past the Crab and Conch Shell and the newsagent's, all the way to the far end, where she found herself looking at— NOTHING! There was only shadow and darkness where the Hippodrome should have been. She was just about to fling the window open to get a better look when lightning parted the sky again – and there it was.

Having been hidden in gloom, the crumbling building flashed into view like a spark for the tiniest of moments. Ella felt hypnotised by the sight of it.

'There you are!' she mumbled, and an instant tingle of fear tickled its way across Ella's skin. Suddenly she didn't want to be standing in the dark. Panic flared in her chest and she had the strange feeling that someone was watching her. Without taking her wide eyes away from where the crooked building stood, Ella fumbled for her lamp. Her fingers felt about her desk, and when they finally found the switch, she clicked it on—

To say that Ella screamed loudly would be like saying it was only a bit rainy outside. As her skull lamp illuminated and the image of Ella's bedroom reappeared in the window, she found herself staring at something that made her stomach flip over and her knees buckle.

There in the reflection, standing next to the bookshelves where Ella had placed the little stone hand, was . . . was . . . the young woman from the theatre!

When Ella had spotted her earlier that day, the ballerina hadn't noticed her, even though Ella had shouted and waved . . . but now . . . now she was STARING STRAIGHT AT HER.

The girls' eyes met in the frosted-up glass and Ella felt a rush of fright and exhilaration explode through her veins like the lightning that flashed outside across the sky. She spun away from the window, ready to confront the stranger in her room, frantically opening her mouth to yell and—

Nothing . . .

Ella shook her head and blinked, as if trying to wake herself up from a dream. What had just happened? Where was the girl?

'Hello?' Ella called. 'I know you're there!'

No one replied.

Except for Wilson, who'd practically jumped through the ceiling when Ella had screamed, her bedroom was completely empty. There was no way anyone could have hidden themselves that quickly . . . could they?

'Wha—?' Ella panted. Her heart was pounding so heavily she thought it might play a tune on the inside of her ribs. 'Hello? Ballerina? I didn't imagine you . . . I'm sure I didn't!'

Ella walked slowly over to where the girl had been standing and looked about for any signs of her.

'Hello? Please come back!'

It was just then, as she stood shivering on the spot, that the stone hand sitting on the bookshelf caught her eye. With chattering teeth, Ella peered at the little thing. It was exactly where she had left it, only now . . . now – and she couldn't explain how this could possibly be happening – it was covered in delicate spiky ice crystals that crackled in the uneasy silence. *Crick . . . Crick . . . Cruck . . . !*

Ella picked the hand up with trembling fingers and held it close to her chest.

'I'll take you back to the theatre,' she whispered, feeling its coldness bite her skin. 'I promise.'

3
JUST LIKE HER

'Look out!'

Ella had just shuffled sleepily through the kitchen door when a soapy sponge sailed through the air and landed in the sink with a *SPLOOSH!*

'Morning, darling!' Mum beamed. She was kneeling on the tiled floor surrounded by bottles of cleaning liquids, dishcloths and scouring brushes. 'You slept for hours, sleepyhead! It might be Sunday, but we've got jobs to do!'

'Bluh,' Ella yawned in reply. She felt strange and a little dizzy, like someone had reached inside her skull and scrambled her brains with an egg whisk.

'D'you know, I was stuck upstairs with Miss Jenkins for nearly an hour last night! I had to make the old grump about twenty cups of tea to say sorry for losing some of her nibbly bits in the rain.' Mum hauled a bucket of dirty water over to the sink and poured it away. 'When I finally got back down here, you were fast asleep, darling. You didn't even have any dinner. Are you feeling all right? I'd hate for you to catch a cold.'

Ella wasn't listening. She rubbed her bleary eyes and tried to sift through the milkshake of memories gurgling around in her head. What happened? Had she dreamed up the girl in her room? Ella couldn't even remember getting into bed or going to sleep. A spine-snapping image of the ballerina pirouetted across her thoughts and—

'Mind yourself – I'm still cleaning.' Mum nudged Ella aside as she started whizzing about the floor with the mop. 'Now, darling, I need you to pop into town for me again this morning. Is that okay?'

Ella stared out of the kitchen window, searching for a view of the theatre through the chimneypots, but the fog was back, thicker than before.

'Ella?'

Maybe the ballerina had followed her home? But how had she got into her bedroom, and where had she vanished to so quickly?

'ELLA!'

'Huh?' Ella jumped, and found Mum standing right in front of her, looking concerned.

'I'm talking to you, silly,' Mum said. She placed a hand on Ella's forehead and checked her temperature.

'Are you sure you're feeling all right?'

Ella shrugged Mum away. 'I'm just a bit sleepy,' she said with an unconvincing smile. 'That's all. I'm good.'

'It must be the excitement of living in Cod's Bottom,' Mum replied, before planting a kiss on top of Ella's head. 'But now you're back in the land of the living, do you mind running into town for me today? I need you to get a few things from the shops.'

'That's fine,' Ella replied, shaking off the last of her grogginess. A tiny spark of delight had ignited in her belly at the thought of wandering into Cod's Bottom by herself. 'I want to head back to the theatre anyway.'

'To the Hippodrome?' Mum asked, her face falling into an instant frown.

'Yep! I'm going to have a good look around,' Ella said. 'There's someone inside I want to talk to.'

'What do you mean?'

'I'm going to head to the theatre and—'

'You can't!' Mum snapped.

'I'm just going to have a quick look around and find the dancer girl—'

'Out of the question,' Mum said, shaking her head.

'Why?'

Mum gently squeezed Ella's shoulders and looked her square in the eye. 'Darling, the Hippodrome is falling down. Do you understand? It's dangerous! I know you miss theatre club, but you can't just go wandering into a dilapidated old building. There's no one in there for you to talk to—'

'There is! The ballerina!'

'Ella Jane Griffin!' Mum practically spat the words out. She only ever used Ella's full name when she meant business. 'Stop it! Now, promise me—'

'What?'

'Promise me you won't go anywhere near that place, Ella. Losing Sylvie this year has been hard enough to deal with. I'm not having you squashed under a collapsing ruin you shouldn't have been nosing around in!'

Ella wanted to argue back, but Mum was pulling her super-serious face and she looked like she might cry.

'I'm not joking, darling,' Mum added after a minute of silence. 'Promise me!'

Ella nodded reluctantly, trying to look as disappointed as she could. Her Saturday theatre club back in London had proved useful for that sort of thing.

'Good.' Mum seemed satisfied. She pulled Ella into a hug and squeezed her. 'You're so like your poor Aunt Sylvie sometimes.'

'Really?' Ella asked.

'Such imaginations! My little sister was exactly the same as you when we were girls. All this talk of ballerinas and poodle ladies . . .'

'Poodle ladies? I didn't mention a poodle lady,' said Ella. 'What are you talking about?'

'Hmm?' Mum grunted, still hugging her daughter tightly.

'I said, I didn't say anything about a poodle lady.'

'Didn't you?' Mum let Ella wriggle free and smiled down at her. 'Oh, what am I saying? That was Sylvie. When we were little, she used to natter on about a ballerina, and there was a lady with some poodles, I seem to remember. They were some sort of imaginary friends of hers, or a game or something . . . I never understood it. Your grandad used to go bonkers, telling her off for visiting that mouldy old place too. You're just the same.'

Ella felt a frizz of excitement on the edges of her thoughts. A ballerina and now a poodle lady?

'Anyway,' Mum sighed, grabbing the mop again and readying herself for more cleaning, 'I've written a shopping list – it's on the fridge. '

'No problem, Mum,' Ella said a little too eagerly. She grabbed the scrap of paper and sprinted back towards her bedroom for her coat.

'AND NO GOING TO THE HIPPODROME!' Mum yelled after her.

But Ella didn't reply.

4
NO ONE SPEAKS TO THEM!

'Frozen peas, sticky tape, hand soap, tomato ketchup, picture hooks, toothpaste . . .' Ella chanted the list to herself as she trudged down Cuttlebone Lane, counting the cobblestones beneath her feet. Wilson trotted along behind. If she was quick, there would be enough time to buy the groceries and run across to the other side of the harbour for another look at the theatre before Mum got suspicious.

'I'm not breaking my promise if I only peek through the gates,' she mumbled to the little dog. 'There's no harm in looking, is there, Wilsy?'

As the narrow alley opened out onto the promenade, Ella turned right for the Laughing Starfish Store, when . . .

'Are you unusual?'

The voice took Ella by surprise and she flinched, then glanced about, trying to spot its owner.

'I don't talk to unusual people, you know.'

Wilson barked and pulled on his lead, spinning Ella round in an instant. She steadied herself as her boots squeaked on the wet pavement and suddenly found herself staring at a figure standing beneath the big noticeboard outside the post office.

'My daddy told me there was a new girl in Cod's Bottom, and I think you're her. Are you unusual though? I want to be certain you're not before we can be friends.'

Ella didn't know how to respond. Her mind had been focused on groceries and the Hippodrome, and now she found herself gawking at the neatest and most perfectly prim girl she'd ever seen. What was going on?

'Veronica Ratsinger,' the girl said, tossing her long dark plaits over each shoulder. She hurried over to Ella, grabbed her by the hand and shook it vigorously. 'My daddy is a town councillor . . . the best one. He makes all the important decisions around here. Can you believe it?'

'Oh . . .' is all Ella replied.

'I live up on the cliffs, not down here in this dump. Yuck!'

Ella said nothing.

'And I go to the finest school in the entire Upper Haddock Norton region – Our Lady Of Cod's Bottom . . .' Veronica paused like she was waiting for applause. 'It's the school YOU should attend, when the summer holidays are over.'

Ella shrugged. Mum hadn't even talked about that stuff yet. 'I don't know . . .' she began.

'You must! Only the best people go there,' Veronica declared. 'We're going to be best friends, I can tell. I'm the smartest girl in the whole town, and not just because of my family, you know. The Ratsingers are better than everyone, but I'm just naturally brilliant on top of that, so you'll definitely want to be my friend. I'm going to be prime minister one day!'

Ella forced a smile and nodded. She'd only met Veronica a second ago and already she was feeling the urge to run away from the sour-faced little brat.

'Don't look so overwhelmed, new girl,' Veronica sneered. 'I know I'm extraordinary, but I'm very friendly . . . even to people who live down here.'

'Um . . .' Ella tried to untie her tongue. She looked at Veronica's impeccable clothes and realised the vinegary girl was dressed in a school uniform. There was a little emblem on the pocket of her blazer with the words *Our Lady of Cod's Bottom* embroidered underneath it. 'Why are you wearing that?' she asked.

'My uniform?' Veronica said with pride. 'Why wouldn't I wear it?'

'It's the summer holidays?'

'One must always strive to impress. That's what my daddy says,' Veronica answered, straightening the hem of her skirt. 'Anyway, I think I should be asking you the same question. Why are *you* wearing *that*? Are you going to a costume party or something in those ugly boots?'

Ella looked down. In her hurry to get dressed and out of the door, she had decided to wear her lime green shirt and yellow dungarees along with her brand-new purple boots. Brightly coloured clothing normally made Ella feel brave – Frida Kahlo had taught her that – but now she suddenly felt embarrassed, like she was sticking out a little too much on the grey harbour. Ella Griffin: the circus clown!

'You do *look* a bit unusual,' Veronica declared. 'I'm still not sure about you. Is that your dog?'

'Yep,' said Ella, feeling a little shaken. 'His name's Wils—'

'Daddy says dogs are dirty creatures,' Veronica said flatly. 'Do you like ponies?'

'I, er . . .' Ella wasn't too keen on ponies, or horses . . . or unicorns for that matter. Anything that pranced really. 'I suppose so,' she lied, hoping it would end the conversation sooner.

Veronica raised an eyebrow. 'How many have you got?'

'None,' Ella mumbled, contemplating making a dive over the harbour wall.

'None? No ponies? Ha!' Veronica re-tossed her plaits over her shoulders. 'I have TWO PONIES. My riding instructor said I should only get one, but Daddy bought me a second pony anyway. I insisted!'

'Oh . . .'

'My daddy is a councillor . . . did I mention that? He's going to transform this stupid little town and be mayor. Look –' Veronica pointed to a large sign pinned to the noticeboard.

VISITORS' MULTISTOREY CAR PARK COMING SOON TO COD'S BOTTOM!

'Then he'll be a member of parliament soon enough,' Veronica went on, practically swooning with smugness. 'And, finally, he'll be prime minister . . . and, when he's finished, I'll take over and run the whole country.'

Ella nodded, trying to appear as if she was still listening to the deluded girl. She didn't care in the slightest about councillors or ponies, and she definitely didn't like this snub-nosed griper. An enormous sense of loneliness suddenly coursed through Ella's body and the urge to cry heaved in her chest. Where were Ava and Yusif when she needed her beasties? They felt further away than ever. *Am I slowly losing everyone I love?* she thought.

'Guess their names!' Veronica whined, snapping Ella away from her worrying.

'What?'

'Guess their names, my ponies!'

'Um . . .' Ella felt her cheeks flush red. 'Betty and . . . er . . . Reginald?'

'Ugh!' Veronica Ratsinger stared at Ella as if she had something revolting dangling from the end of her nose. 'Their names are Poppy Pumpkin and Rainbow Swift! I wouldn't give them STUPID names like Betty and Reginald.'

DON'T LAUGH . . . DON'T LAUGH . . . DON'T LAUGH . . . Ella fought off a grin and decided not to confess that her grandparents were called Betty and Reginald, and those were much better names than . . . what was it – Pimple Stiltskin and Rainy Swamp?

'Anyway,' Veronica said, picking a stray piece of fluff from the cuff of her blazer, 'we're going to be best friends! The last one *had* to go, so I need a new one. And you'll do, I think. We'll spend every day of the summer holidays together and . . . WAIT! WHERE ARE YOU GOING, NEW GIRL?'

Before Ella had even realised what she was doing, she'd yanked on Wilson's lead and bundled the little dog into the Laughing Starfish Store, leaving Veronica Ratsinger moaning behind her on the pavement as the door shut with a loud *TING-A-LING-A-LING!*

Twenty minutes later, after lurking in the aisles for as long as she could between the loo rolls and washing-up liquid bottles, Ella had collected everything on Mum's list and was ready to head outside again.

'Check the coast is clear,' she whispered to herself, like one of the secret spy kids in her favourite *MYSTERY MANIACS* comic books. 'Spot the villain before the villain spots you . . .'

Ella peeked cautiously round the edge of the door and surveyed the gloomy promenade as it stretched away from her. Veronica Ratsinger was nowhere to be seen. She must have got the message and simpered off back to her daddy's palace and her ponies.

'Come on then, Wilsy,' Ella said, huffing a sigh of relief. She stepped out onto the front step, glanced across to the other side of the bay where the theatre was hiding in the fog, and—

'About time!'

Ella gasped and spun round. Veronica was *still* standing beneath her father's blasted sign about the new car park! The corner of the post office had obscured her from view when Ella had done her best spy-scan of the waterfront.

'Come here, QUICK!' Veronica ordered, pointing to a spot on the ground right next to her.

Ella didn't move.

'NOW, NEW GIRL!' Veronica barked. 'It's important!'

Suddenly feeling too nervous to argue with the little scowling volcano in a school uniform, Ella skittered over.

'If you're going to be my best friend – and you ARE going to be my best friend – there are a few things you need to know,' Veronica said. It was like she hadn't even noticed that Ella had run away from her twenty minutes ago. 'Listen carefully, er . . . what's your name?'

'Ella.'

'Ella?!' Veronica barely hid her revulsion. 'Listen, Ella, if you want to be seen with a Ratsinger like me, you've got to be better than everyone else in this boring swamp. Daddy insists it's the only way to truly get ahead in life.'

Ella opened her mouth to speak . . . closed it . . . opened it again, but no words came out. If all the children in Cod's Bottom were like Veronica, she was going to spend the rest of her childhood without any friends at all.

'See those two?' Veronica pointed to a couple heading towards them along the cobbles. 'That's Mr and Mrs Ghurai. They're fishmongers.' Veronica pulled a face as if to say that being a fishmonger was the most unimpressive thing in the world. 'Can you imagine spending all day elbow-deep in sardine kegs? Daddy says I'll never work in a shop with little people like that. It's beneath me . . .'

Ella shook her head in disbelief, but Veronica didn't notice. Aunt Sylvie had worked in a shop before she . . . well, before. Who did this spiteful little zit of a girl think she was? The queen?

'That one is Mrs Markham,' Veronica continued, pointing as more people went past. 'We don't mix with the likes of the Markhams. Her granddaughter is in my class and we spotted her picking her nose behind the climbing frame at lunchtime. Disgusting! It should be illegal.'

'That's not very ni—' Ella tried to snap back at

Veronica, but the unkind child was on a roll and clearly had no intention of stopping now.

'Those three oddballs over by the pier perform plays for each other. Freaks!'

Ella's ears pricked up. *What did Veronica just say?*

'They think they're Shakespeare or something. Daddy says that wafty-lofty-artsy types like that will never be successful when they grow up. He thinks that creativity is a waste of brain cells.'

'Who performs plays?' Ella asked, looking around. She'd completely lost her patience with Veronica's stupid prattling. How could creativity EVER be a waste of brain cells? It was certain . . . Veronica Ratsinger was a complete and utter bum-face, but the kids who liked Shakespeare sounded brilliant.

'Those three over by the pier,' Veronica whispered back as she pretended to be quietly reading the flyers on the noticeboard. 'Complete losers. No one talks to them. Don't let them see you looking or they might come over. I'd never live it down!'

Ella squinted through the rolling fog and spotted three children a little way off, jumping about on a bench near the entrance to the pier.

'That one is Nula Wilkes.' Veronica pointed at the nearest girl and sneered. 'She's definitely unusual.'

Ella peered at the girl and suddenly longed to

wave at her. She liked the bright scarf tied round Nula's curly hair and thought her colourful friendship bracelets looked fun. Ella wished she had fancy things like that.

'Bertie Gripes is more than unusual – he's peculiar.' Veronica continued, nodding at a boy who was diving over the back of the bench. He was short for his age, had a round freckly face, and wore a piece of red fabric tied over his jumper like a cape. 'Daddy doesn't approve of boys who play with girls.'

Well, your daddy sounds like an idiot! Boys who play with girls are the BEST KIND! Ella wanted to say, but she just ignored Veronica's mean comments and stayed silent. She loved Bertie's cape and had one just like it in her dressing-up box at home, only hers was green.

'And the third one –' Veronica pointed to the other girl who was wearing a skull-and-crossbones T-shirt and sported a pirate hat over her short pixie haircut – 'is Violet Bunkly. Imagine having a name like that?!'

Feeling relieved to know that there were children like this in Cod's Bottom, Ella almost cheered out loud. It was just then, as she gazed at the raucous trio, that the fog parted and Bertie spotted her. He smiled across the promenade. Ella smiled back and felt warm for the first time since she'd arrived in town. A tiny pinprick of hope sparkled somewhere in the back of her brain. Maybe *they* would be her friends? She certainly wasn't planning on becoming the sidekick of vicious Veronica Ratsinger any time soon.

The girl named Violet twisted as she jumped off the pier railing, and Ella spotted a Frida Kahlo patch sewn onto the sleeve of her top.

'AH!' Ella had to grip her toes and clench her bottom to stop herself from whooping.

'Don't they look gross?' Veronica scoffed. 'Really stupid!'

Ella didn't reply, unable to tear her eyes away from the three children. Right then and there, she made a secret plan to get to know them as soon as possible. She just had to get rid of Veronica first . . .

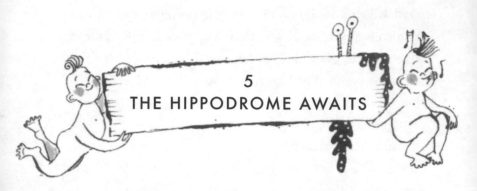

5
THE HIPPODROME AWAITS

'You're coming back to my house!' Veronica told Ella, after the other three children's game took them further along the seafront and out of sight through the sea mist. 'I live on top of the cliff where all the big houses are, but it's okay for you to visit if you're with me. You can meet Poppy Pumpkin and Rainbow Swift, and then we can watch my favourite film. It's about a princess who freezes everything and builds an ice palace, and conjures up a new dress, and—'

'No!' Ella blurted a little too quickly. 'I can't!'

Veronica scowled. 'Why not? You're supposed to be my best friend. I'll tell my daddy!'

'I would . . . I mean I'd love to visit your home. That sounds like *so* much fun,' Ella said through gritted teeth. 'Only . . . only . . .'

Veronica's face creased itself into the most alarming

pout Ella had ever seen. She turned as pink as the ribbons at the ends of her plaits and looked like she was chewing a hornets' nest!

'Only Mum is washing my hair with nit shampoo this afternoon.' Ella finished her sentence off with a giant grin. She twitched her eyebrows mischievously as she lifted the grocery bag in her hand. 'That's what I was buying. We'll get the little blighters eventually. Mum's convinced it'll work this time around.'

Quicker than she could have yelled *GET AWAY FROM ME, FLEABAG!* Veronica recoiled from Ella like she was holding a tarantula and waving it about.

'EURGH!!!' she shrieked. 'YOU'VE GOT NITS?'

'Not for long!' Ella beamed. 'If Mum can't wash them out, I'll just pass them on to someone else soon. That always does the trick.'

'AAAAGGGHHHHH!!!' Veronica Ratsinger flew backwards against the noticeboard like she had springs in the bottom of her perfectly polished shoes. She screamed again, turned a sickly shade of pale green, then sprinted away across the promenade, flapping her arms up and down like a panic-stricken chicken. 'DISGUSTING! *DADDY* – SHE'S UNUSUAL AFTER ALL!'

'Oh no! Come back, please! They're only little nits. TINY, FRIENDLY ONES!' Ella giggled and waved as Veronica vanished through the fog. She listened as the sound of yelping and sobbing faded into the distance.

'Perfect!' That ought to keep Veronica away for a while. Ella sighed to herself, then gave Wilson's lead a little tug. 'Come on, Wilsy – let's go and see where those children went.'

Stepping carefully across the wonky cobbles, trying not to slip, Ella had dragged Wilson as far as the wool shop when . . .

'NEEEOOOORRR! I c-can fly faster than you! *POW!*'

Ella stopped in her tracks, peering along the misty seafront. She could just make out Bertie Gripes standing outside the newsagent's up ahead, swishing his red cape and jumping about like he was dodging invisible lasers.

'No one can b-beat me!'

Ella sidestepped into a doorway, then peeked back round the corner at the twirling boy.

'Impossible! My robotic bones are equipped with rocket blasters and splurge cannons!' The girl with the pixie haircut and Frida Kahlo patch – Violet, was it? – leaped onto the road and struck some impressive superhero poses. 'I'll be victorious!'

'NE-NEV-NEVER!'

They both rolled around, hollering and laughing, while Ella watched on in silence. She quickly picked

Wilson up with one arm to stop him barking and drawing attention. Why was she hiding? These were the kids she'd sworn to meet, weren't they? Ella sighed to herself. She suddenly felt extremely silly for ducking out of sight, but there was nothing she could do about it now except stay hidden.

She watched as the third child, Nula Wilkes, jumped out of the newsagent's, turned to the door and shouted, 'BYE, MUM!' Then all three superheroes ran in the opposite direction, off towards the far end of the sea wall and . . .

'The theatre!' Ella gasped. She stepped back out onto the promenade, put Wilson down and felt her heart beginning to race. The newsagent's was the last shop on the seafront. Beyond that were just piles of foul-smelling fishing nets and the cliff path. 'They're heading to the theatre!'

She didn't have time to think. In an instant Ella started running as fast as she could along the crooked arc of the harbour wall, past the fish shop and the Crab and Conch Shell pub, slipping and sliding over the uneven road as she sprinted.

'This is our chance!' Ella panted to Wilson as they narrowly missed a man carrying a crate of stinking sardines across the fishermen's yard. 'Run, run, run!'

Ahead, Ella could just about see the three children

standing next to the tall angels by the gates. Maybe one of them had the keys for the padlock?

'Wait!' Ella yelled, but she was short of breath and it came out as a wheeze. *Ugh!* Why wasn't she better at running? 'Please wait!' Ella wanted to wave her arms about like Veronica Ratsinger escaping from her dreaded nits, but with Wilson's lead in one hand and the paper bag of groceries in the other, that was impossible. 'I'm right behind y—' Ella glanced back up from the shopping in her arms and found that Nula, Bertie and Violet were no longer standing where she'd glimpsed them a moment ago.

'Hello?' This was getting annoying. Why did people in this odd town always appear suddenly and then completely vanish?

Ella finally reached the gate, red-faced and out of breath. Wilson puffed and snuffled behind her. She peered through the rusted bars but there was no sign of her superhero future friends.

'Hello? It's Ella Griffin. I'm new in Cod's Bottom. Can you hear me?' she called, but nobody replied. Only the cherubs above the theatre entrance seemed to have noticed her and stared curiously.

Ella put her shopping bag down next to Wilson at the feet of one of the angels, then shook the gate as hard as she could. It squeaked a little but didn't open.

'OW!' Ella instantly regretted giving the middle bar a hefty kick. She shook the gate again, but the chain was still wrapped round its middle and the rusted padlock clearly hadn't been unlocked in a very long time.

'*Hmmm* . . . where did they go?' she muttered to herself, then remembered her *MYSTERY MANIACS* comic books and started searching for clues.

'Can you sniff them out, Wilsy?' Ella said, looking around. 'No?' Wilson snorted and rolled onto his back with his paws in the air. 'Didn't think so.' She chuckled as she bent down to scratch his tummy. 'You have other talents, don't you?'

Crouching, Ella glanced downwards and smiled when she saw lots of wet footprints in the mud, just on the other side of the metal bars. She wasn't sure how they'd managed, but it looked like Nula, Bertie and Violet must have gone through the gate, even though it was locked.

'Found you!' she murmured. 'So, how'd you do it?'

Ella stood up and was just starting to examine the lock when she was startled by a voice on the other side.

'I heard she moved here from London.'

Ella ducked against the stone archway and secretly watched through the bars as Nula and Bertie came marching round the side of the theatre and heaved open one of its red-and-gold doors with their shoulders.

'Ha ha! The new girl t-told Ratsinger she had nits. Veronica was screaming about it.' Bertie chuckled. 'Genius! I th-think she sounds fun.'

'Veronica will be wailing and gnashing for a week,' Nula continued before stepping into the inky shadows beyond the theatre's entrance. 'She looked terrified! That'll teach her, the nasty bully!'

Ella gasped. They were talking about her!

'I *sound fun*,' she whispered to herself, barely able to control her enormous grin. 'Bertie thinks I'm a . . . a genius!' After the past few miserable days, this was a wonderful thing to hear.

'Even if you spotted the new girl here yesterday, Nula, we can't invite her in.' Violet's words interrupted Ella's thoughts as she walked into view and followed her friends inside. 'It's too risky. The Hippodrome has to stay secret.'

This was it! Ella could barely control her excitement. Now she knew there were children who visited the theatre, there was nothing that could stop her from joining them!

She quickly went about testing the crooked railings on both sides of the gates, pushing and pulling, searching for something loose.

'One of them has to budge,' she grunted as she gave each metal bar a hefty shove in turn. 'Come on . . .'

She rattled another. Nothing.

'There has to be . . .'

The next bar didn't wobble at all.

'. . . a way . . .'

The third bar groaned, but stayed where it was.

'IN!'

Ella pushed on the fourth bar with all her weight. She wedged her shoulder against it, scraped her purple boots across the cobbles, and pushed.

'LET ME IN— *AAAAARGHHHH!*'

With a loud *CLUNK* of metal, the loose bar moved and Ella found herself suddenly stumbling forwards, flailing her arms and bracing herself for the inevitable muddy *SPLAT!* that rushed up to meet her on the other side of the gate.

'Ugh! I knew it!' Ella grunted, face down in sticky brown sludge. She scrambled to her feet, her heart pounding, and quickly checked around to make sure no one had seen her face-flop into the mud like a bewildered toad in yellow dungarees.

Whatever Ella was about to say vanished into the wind as she looked up and saw the Cod's Bottom Hippodrome looming above her. Her mouth gaped open and her ribs heaved with excitement. On this side of the gate, the building suddenly seemed ten times bigger and far more impressive, like a crooked, weather-beaten galleon that had washed onto the rocks in some dreadful Cod's Bottom squall.

'Hello?' Ella said quietly. She met the stare of a gaggle of cherubs sitting along the edge of an upper-floor balcony. Hadn't their little stone faces all been turned towards the sea before? Ella shook her head and steadied her nerves. Of course stone cherubs don't shift their gaze . . . she was just being silly.

The theatre moaned a greeting through its many jagged-toothed windows and Ella jolted at the sound. Resisting the impulse to write another list, she slid her fingers back into her pocket and touched the tiny stone hand lying in its folds. She mustn't forget to find its rightful owner later, but first . . .

She scrambled to her feet, turned back to the gate, grabbed the end of Wilson's lead through the bars and tied it tightly to one of the sturdy railings.

'You stay here, Wilsy, and guard the shopping. I won't be long.'

Then Ella began searching for a way through the overgrown thicket that stood between her and the theatre. There must be a gap somewhere. If she hurried, Nula, Bertie and Violet wouldn't have got too far ahead and she'd catch up with them.

'Seek out the clues and follow your nose,' she declared, trying again to act exactly like one of the superspies from her comic books. 'Aha—!'

It didn't take Ella long to spot more muddy footprints, which she began to follow as fast as she could through the prickly bushes.

'Don't stop now, Ella Griffin,' she commanded herself. A strange nervousness bubbled up inside her, and Ella knew she *had* to meet these new children before she felt too shy to even think about turning back. 'It's watching princess films with Veronica Ratsinger for you if you don't make some real friends. Go!'

In no time, Ella had followed the line of footprints straight up to the red-and-gold doors. She raised a hand to touch the crumbling wood and— *Brrr!* Ella's spine juddered as the theatre moaned again in the breeze. The sound was deep and eerie and made the hairs on the back of her neck stand on end. *Come in*, it seemed to sigh in a language all of its own, and its theatre-breath smelled of dust and motheaten carpets. *Ella, come in! The Hippodrome awaits!*

Without glancing back, Ella stood up straight, clenched her fists and stepped through the peeling doorway into the thick and smothering darkness.

6
DANCING IN THE DARK

Floorboards
creaked beneath
Ella's feet and dust
clouds drifted away
from her as she fumbled
nervously into the Hippodrome.
Her heart was pounding and her
fingers trembled uncontrollably. The
old building was so much gloomier than
Ella had expected and . . .

'COR!' was all she managed to blurt as her eyes eventually adjusted to the dark. A million fantastic sights began to emerge as the shadows crept back to their hiding places. Ella's stomach did a cartwheel. It was always much better at cartwheeling than she was.

A wide vestibule unfolded around her, and this led into the grand foyer of the theatre. She had never seen anything so . . . so . . . Ella couldn't think of exactly the right word, so she just whispered, *'Wonderful!'* The rickety remains of a box office and a cloakroom stood either side of her, where customers from long ago had hustled and bustled about before heading through into an enormous atrium. It was SPECTACULAR!

Ella snatched her trusty green notebook and pen from her coat pocket and started scribbling every detail down as fast as she could.

Before her was a vast circular room with a marble floor patterned in greens and pinks. Tall pillars stood around the edges and, overhead, squillions of little cherubs like the ones she'd seen outside surrounded ornate glass lamps. Straight ahead, a wide staircase covered in threadbare red carpet swooped up and spiralled around to the floor above. Its gold, swirly banister was knotted with cobwebs, feathers and dried leaves blown in through the broken windows. All of it was . . . beautiful!

'I'LL BEAT YOU!'

A voice suddenly broke through the quiet and made Ella practically jump out of her muddy dungarees. It belonged to Bertie.

'NOT IF I GET THERE FIRST!' Violet's voice replied. 'I ALWAYS WIN!'

The children's laughter echoed in every direction through the foyer, bouncing off walls and pillars, making it sound as if there were people all around Ella.

'Hello?' she called quietly back, not wanting to be any noisier. It felt as if the building might collapse if she yelled too loudly. 'Hello? Can you hear me?'

Ella walked out into the centre of the circular floor, looked up and gasped.

There, high above her in the middle of the atrium's ceiling hung a colossal chandelier made from more crystals than Ella could ever count. It was broken and wonky and had become the roost of hundreds of generations of pigeons, but even with the strands of grime and spiderwebs that dangled from it, the thing was amazing to look at. It was bigger than Mum's car!

Laughter echoed around the giant room again and a few birds went flurrying about, making the chandelier jangle and sway, casting twinkling dots of light all over the place.

'Hello?' Ella called, more determined this time. 'It's Ella Griffin! I'm new!'

She stuffed her green notebook back into her coat pocket. Bertie, Nula and Violet were clearly playing on one of the higher floors, and if Ella wanted to find them, she'd have to follow their voices.

Crrreeaak! Crrruuunnnch! Crrraaack!

'Please, don't break,' Ella pleaded as she made her way up the staircase. The thing was so old, its last strands of red carpet were disintegrating to dust under her feet. 'I only want to get to the next floor.'

Please get off me! the staircase groaned back, but Ella didn't speak Staircase, so she ignored it and kept going.

Crrreeeaaak! Crrraaaccck! Snnnaaap!

Ella placed one purple-booted foot onto the first-floor landing and breathed a deep sigh. She'd made it.

'Hello?' she called again. 'Nula? Bertie? Violet? I don't mean to interrupt, but I saw you all come in and I . . . I love theatres. I want to be an actor one day.'

Still nothing.

Ella walked a little further, testing for weak spots as she looked around. In front of her, a gallery curved round the edge of the first floor, looking down on the atrium below. There were two large double doors either side of it and, if Ella wasn't mistaken, through them she'd find the . . . the . . . ugh! She'd forgotten the word.

Grumbling to herself, Ella grabbed her green notebook again and flicked to a page where she'd listed all the parts of a theatre she'd visited back in London last year.

Box office (where you buy tickets)
Foyer (big entrance hall)
Cloakroom (where you leave your
    coats or even your cloaks)
Bar (lemonade for me, glass of
    wine for Mum)
Auditorium
Balcony
Boxes (little balconies for fancy-
    pants people)
The Proscenium arch (the BIG
    arch above the stage)
The stage (TA-DAH!)

'The auditorium!' Ella said. That was the word she'd been looking for. Through those big double doors she'd find the auditorium, the great room filled with seats, where people would have sat to watch plays and pantomimes, ballets, musicals and operas. If *she* was Nula, Bertie or Violet, that's exactly where *she* would go to play.

She walked up to the nearest set of doors and readied herself excitedly. Taking hold of the brass door handle, Ella felt a buzz of anticipation tingle its way from her toes up to her head. This was it – her plans were all happening at once. She'd find new friends and explore a really-real theatre all at the same time!

'HELLOOOO!' Ella yanked open the door and beamed her best smile. She felt sure her soon-to-be-friends would love a grand entrance, so she jumped forwards and flung her arms wide, like a gameshow host on the telly. 'IT'S ME! ELLA GRIF—'

Ella had been right about some things, but wrong about others.

She'd found the auditorium all right. At least, she thought she had. Wherever she was, it was huge, dark and cold. But there was no sign of the three children.

'Where are you, guys?' Ella groaned, but she soon forgot about Nula, Bertie and Violet as her eyes started to readjust once more to the deep, damp-smelling darkness that had wrapped itself round her.

With the doors swinging closed behind Ella, the only light was a thin shaft from some unseen crack in the ceiling above, slicing through the crumbling auditorium ahead of her. She was standing in one of the huge balconies looking down on rows and rows of empty motheaten seats that all faced towards . . . This time, Ella definitely knew the word for what she saw.

The proscenium! A big archway carved with more mischievous cherubs, lounging angels and meddling gods arced its way up and over the stage.

'There it is!' Ella squeaked with excitement. 'The stage!'

There was so much to look at that Ella didn't know where to start. She could make out old painted-scenery cloths fluttering in the gloom and tattered curtains hanging in disarray over the warped and splintered stage-boards. There were bent instruments and a broken piano visible in one corner, and the remains of a wicker hamper with bits of costumes spilling out of it on the other.

'I must have been wrong before. I bet *that's* where they go to play.'

The echoes of Bertie and Violet's laughter earlier must have confused her and made her think they were upstairs. That *had* to be what happened! She decided to head back down and find a way into the lower part of the theatre if she was going to meet her future friends, but, as Ella turned to leave, something caught her eye.

She froze.

Into the narrow shaft of light, just where it hit the buckled stage floor, stepped the ballerina she'd spotted in the window yesterday. Ella stared and felt goosebumps creep across her skin. She thought about calling out, but something stopped her and she decided to watch on in silence.

The ballerina paused in the light and almost seemed to shimmer for a moment, then drew herself up, as tall and delicate as a snowflake. She slowly raised her arms and began to dance.

Ella was instantly transfixed.

The girl glided and twirled across the stage and, with her, a violin started playing. Its haunting music dipped and swooped as she leaped and pirouetted this way and that, but Ella couldn't see where the tune was coming from. She *didn't care* where it was coming from. A real-life ballerina was performing right in front of her, and Ella's heart was practically dancing every step alongside.

She sighed to herself but, in the darkness, failed to notice her breath coming out as a cloud. The vast room had suddenly grown gravely cold, and although Ella couldn't see it, ice crystals had started to crackle across the walls behind her and all along the brass handrail she was leaning against.

Tears welled up in Ella's eyes as the beautiful girl kicked and fluttered to the sad sound of the violin. She moved like smoke, weaving her way across the uneven boards, jumping and sliding, until . . .

There was a tiny second when Ella didn't quite

understand what she was seeing. She blinked in alarm and gripped the handrail to steady herself, finding it covered in tiny icicles.

The ballerina twisted and spiralled towards the front of the stage, and just when it had looked like she was about to tumble straight off the edge and fall into the orchestra pit, she gently floated out over the rows of seats, drifting higher and higher as her dance whirled onwards and upwards into the dust-filled air.

7
SO THAT'S THEIR SECRET!

'I told you I heard something! WHAT ARE YOU DOING HERE?' a voice screamed, but it wasn't coming from Ella or the ballerina drifting overhead.

Ella, who had been frozen to the spot with terror, spun round and nearly exploded into a million petrified pieces. Her eyes couldn't see straight in her confusion, and she thrashed her arms wildly, scrabbling at nothing but darkness.

'GET OUT!' the voice continued to shout. 'WHY ARE YOU HERE?'

Ella turned again, and this time she found something to focus on in the shadows. There, standing in the double doorway with a surprised look on her face, was Violet.

'Who are you?' the pixie-haired girl yelled, squinting to see more clearly. 'Come into the light!'

Ella didn't need to be asked twice, but she also had

no intention of sticking around while a ballerina was pirouetting over the balconies and floating through the air. She sprinted towards Violet, bawling and yelping, then barged her aside and staggered back out onto the first-floor landing.

'New girl?' Violet gasped as Ella somehow steadied herself mid-sprint and clattered towards the top of the staircase. 'Come back!'

Ella was in a frenzy of fear. Her heart was pounding like a steam engine, powering her feet to KEEP RUNNING.

'What's g-going on?' Bertie called out before Ella had time to spot him. She practically dived down the first few rickety steps and it was only as she thundered round their sweeping curve, too fast to stop, that she saw the boy standing on the stairs below her.

Ella opened her mouth to scream *MOVE!* but the only thing that escaped between her teeth was another horrified croak.

'Hi!' the boy cheered when he saw her coming. Bertie smiled, then realised Ella was about to squish him in a one-girl stampede and he lunged out of the way instead. 'Wait! W-what's happening?'

Too many thoughts were whizzing around in Ella's mind at once. She felt awful for barging Violet aside and for nearly flattening Bertie, but every instinct she had

71

was telling her to get out of the Hippodrome and never return.

'*OOOF!*' Without glancing up, Ella bounded off the last step and ran face-first into Nula, who was crossing the foyer on her way towards the staircase. The two girls landed in a knot of wriggling limbs and sore foreheads, right in the middle of the marble floor.

'OW!' Nula lay there whimpering for a moment, her eyes shut, then squirmed out from under Ella, pushed herself up onto her elbows and grimaced. 'My head! Bertie, was that—?'

Nula finally opened her eyes and gawped. 'NEW GIRL!?!'

That was it. Ella's legs seemed to be reacting faster than her brain could. In seconds, she was back on her feet and hurtling for the red-and-gold doors at the front of the theatre.

'Oh, what a lot of fuss!' a voice chortled behind Ella as she ran. Ella couldn't be sure if she was imagining things in all the craziness, but it sounded like it came from a much older woman. 'I sense she's leaving.'

'So disappointing,' came a second voice. This one definitely belonged to a man. 'I felt sure she'd like to hear my poetry.'

'Of course she wouldn't,' laughed another. 'She's just another cowardly Cod's Bottomer. They're all the same.'

'She might like to hear one of my witty ditties though!'

'Cheeky if you ask me . . .'

Ella reached the doors and, just before she charged through them, curiosity bit her on the shoulder – and she glanced back towards the foyer.

There stood Violet, Bertie and Nula near the bottom of the steps, and all around them were . . . she couldn't understand it . . . all around the three children were lots of other people, or at least the *shape* of lots of other people, huddled in groups on the staircase. They seemed to be see-through and shimmering, and Ella found she couldn't quite focus on them. They were there and not there at the same time, like when you look at a light bulb then close your eyes, and you can still see its image on the back of your eyelids.

Ella didn't know how to explain what she was seeing, but one word flashed across her thoughts—

'GHOSTS!!!'

Ice crystals crackled across Ella's heart and, for the second time in two days, she ran away from the Cod's Bottom Hippodrome as fast as she could.

8
NEVER GOING OUTSIDE AGAIN!

Ella sat on her bed and hugged her knees. It was breakfast time, but she wasn't hungry, plus there were some jelly beans stashed in her desk drawer in case of emergencies, so she definitely wasn't planning on leaving her room any time soon.

Three days had passed since she'd run away from the Hippodrome, and Ella had spent that whole time pretending to be ill, barcly leaving her bedroom. She looked at the window and the grey sky beyond it, then shivered.

'I think I *must* be bonkers,' she said to Wilson, who was snoozing on her stripy-socked feet. 'Proper loop-de-loop bonkers.'

No matter how many times Ella had replayed the scene of the flying ballerina and the chattering, there-but-not-quite-there people on the stairs, she just couldn't make sense of it. Had she imagined it? Maybe Veronica Ratsinger was right and she was a total weirdo.

'They couldn't really be g-gho-ghos . . . g-guh . . .' There was no way Ella was going to say it out loud. Everything felt strange and scary. 'G-gho . . . they're not real!'

She glanced down at her open notebook and reread the list she'd made on Sunday after seeing the g-gho . . . the gho-ghos . . . *them*, to try and make sense of things.

What I Know I Think I Did

Met Veronica Ratsinger.

Saw Nula, Bertie and Violet.

Followed Nula, Bertie and Violet to the theatre.

Explored.

Saw ballerina.

Ballerina FLEW!?!?

Ran like crazy.

Saw see-through people.

Collected Wilsy at theatre gate.
(But forgot the shopping.)

Legged it home.

Mum furious.

Hidden in room for two days straight.

Third morning here now. Planning to hide today too.

Ella groaned to herself and flopped back down on the bed. It had been a super-strange turn of events, but now . . . ? Now she was stuck in her room for the third day in a row and hadn't been back into town or seen the three children again. Things were boring but safe . . .

Ella knew she wouldn't be able to stay indoors for ever. Mum never let her have more than a day or two of sickly slouching in her room. Plus, Mum was SO angry that Ella had stayed out way too long and come home empty-handed that she'd practically had smoke shooting out of her ears. It was unlikely Ella would get away with another bedroom day, but she had her fingers crossed.

'You can do this,' she reassured herself, putting her trusty notebook back into her bedside drawer.

On Sunday, she'd managed to convince Mum that there was a perfectly good reason for showing up late from the shops looking like a wild-haired sweaty mess.

'I'm really poorly!' Ella had sobbed on the doorstep of Minerva Mansions, coughing and spluttering dramatically. 'I sat down to rest and a seagull stole the groceries!'

Thankfully, Mum had believed her after a lot of very good acting (even if she said so herself), and Ella had spent the last two days reading comics, occasionally having a worried cry under the bed or watching dog videos on Mum's battered laptop. If she performed really well, maybe she could get away with it again today.

'Darling!' Mum's voice was suddenly outside the door. It swung open and Mum backed into the room, carrying a tray with buttered crumpets and a glass of orange juice on it. 'Morning, my little sick patient!'

OH NO! Panic flared up in Ella's stomach. She hadn't had time to do her usual 'Indoor Day' preparations! Ella glanced at the thermometer Mum had left on the bedside table and grimaced. Normally, if Ella was pretending to be unwell, she'd make sure to hold the thermometer against the radiator, then jump into bed and pop it into her mouth just as she heard Mum coming.

'Is that you, Mum?' Ella croaked in a raspy whisper, theatrically slumping onto the duvet. She did a few of her best coughs and wheezes. 'I think I must have fainted.'

'Oh, gosh!' Mum said, trying to hide a smirk. She'd become an expert at spotting when Ella was faking and had already sussed things out a whole day ago. 'Shall we take your temperature?'

Mum put the breakfast tray on the desk, then grabbed the thermometer.

'NO! There's no need,' Ella replied with a whimper. 'I'm so . . . so ill.'

'Hmmm, let's see, shall we?' and before Ella had had time to clamp her teeth shut, Mum had stuck the thermometer into her mouth. 'Hopefully it won't be dreadful news.'

Ella nodded, acting like it hurt every bone in her body to do so, and tried desperately to think warm thoughts. *Come on, Ella*, she told herself. *You're boiling hot! You're a volcano! You're a steaming kettle. You're—*

Mum pulled the thermometer back out of Ella's mouth, glanced at it, then sat down on the end of the bed.

'Darling . . .'

'The end is near!' Ella rasped. 'I won't survive if I leave this room.'

'Darling . . .'

'Tell Ava and Yusif I love them. I think I need to stay in bed for at least five years!'

'Ella—' Mum raised an eyebrow and rolled her eyes. 'Yes?'

'There's no hope! You're a goner! We're going to have to put you in the bin or feed you to Miss Jenkins upstairs.'

'Wha—?' Ella knew Mum had caught her out before she'd even finished saying the word.

'You're completely fine! I knew you were. I let you get away with it for two whole days, but enough is enough.'

It was no use. Ella stopped her death-croaks and

looked at Mum with an irritated *HUMPH!*

'If you knew, why didn't you say something?'

'Because I could tell you needed a bit of a break,' Mum said, stroking Ella's cheek. 'You looked dreadful on Sunday. All wide-eyed, like you'd seen a ghost.'

'I suppose I did.'

'It's understandable,' Mum said, smiling sweetly. 'Town was a bit weird and frightening, hmm? Did you get yourself into a panic?'

'You could say that,' Ella mumbled after a few seconds. Why was Mum so good at sniffing out fibs?

'I get it.' Mum reached over and smoothed Ella's hair. 'But you mustn't tell lies.'

Ella felt her cheeks flushing pink.

'Don't forget, I was young once too. I was about your age when I moved to Cod's Bottom,' Mum continued. 'Nanny and Grandad bought this place and we had to start all over again. Sylvie was so good at making new friends, but I remember thinking it was all very daunting. I pretended to be sick for days just so I didn't have to go out and face meeting strangers.'

'Thanks, Mum,' Ella said. She sighed and sensed another cry coming on. Any minute now. Five . . . four . . . three . . . Ella could feel the tears welling up in her eyes and a hefty sob heaving its way to her chest. Two . . . one . . . She opened her mouth and bawled, 'I'm sorry I lied, but it's horrible here and I miss my beasties in London. There's a girl called Veronica Ratsinger, and I got stuck with her outside the post office, and she bullies everyone, and she said my boots are ugly, and she wears her school uniform even in the summer holidays, and she likes PONIES and films about ice princesses, and I told her I have nits to make her leave me alone; and there are three other kids, and . . . and—'

Ella stopped herself mid-sentence before she said anything about the theatre and all the terrifying things that had happened on Sunday.

Mum chuckled then planted a kiss on Ella's head and hugged her tightly. 'It's all right. I know how you feel. Ratsinger, did you say?'

Ella nodded.

'Yikes! That family were making people miserable around here when I was a kid too. Some things never change . . .'

'So . . . can I stay with you today?' Ella asked hopefully. 'I'll help you do the boring jobs, and make lunch. I'll even go upstairs and check on Miss Jenkins.'

Mum tucked the thermometer into her pocket. She stood slowly and walked to the door, then turned and smiled.

'No, Ella,' she said. 'Eat your breakfast and get

dressed. I need you to head to the post office and deliver a letter for me.'

'Oh, please! Veronica might be there!'

'No, Ella. You can't hide in your room for the rest of your life. What did Aunt Sylvie always tell you, hmm?'

'Be brave,' Ella mumbled, glancing over at Sylvie's beautiful face in the framed photograph on her bookshelf. Mum was right. Sylvie was always fearless and never shied away from anything. She wouldn't have hidden in her room.

'And was Frida a scaredy-cat or a fierce rebel-lady?' Mum asked, nodding at Ella's Frida Kahlo picture.

'She was fierce,' Ella replied reluctantly.

'Exactly! So stop fussing. And if you run into a Ratsinger, just tell them to leave you alone,' Mum said. 'Anyway, your friends want to chat to you.'

'Ava and Yusif!?' Ella jumped out of bed. 'Did they call?'

'No, silly. Your new friends. They knocked earlier and they're still outside waiting for you. Go and play, but don't forget to deliver my letter. And DON'T be late for dinner!'

9
NEW FRIENDS

Ella tiptoed down the stairs and thought she might be sick . . . or pee her pants . . . or both!

WHAT ARE THEY DOING HERE?

Feeling more stupid than she'd ever felt in her life, Ella spied through the window at the side of the front door and saw Nula, Bertie and Violet sitting on the pavement just outside. She desperately wished she had superpowers to control their minds and make them all leave.

'Please go,' Ella whispered to them. This was all wrong! The last time Ella had seen these children, she'd run into them – and away from them – gabbling and squawking like a petrified turkey on Christmas morning because she thought she'd seen a gho . . . a gho . . . and now they'd probably come to make fun of her. 'Go away!'

Ella ducked away from the window and was just

about to make a break back towards the staircase when a shrill and very angry-sounding voice bellowed behind her.

'Get out of my way!' Ella spun round to see a tiny old woman coming downstairs on her squeaky stairlift, a pair of walking sticks gripped in her gnarled fingers and a face that would shatter icebergs. She wore a neat dress with a knitted purple cardigan over the top and a matching hat, which looked uncannily like a velvet biscuit tin perched on her head. 'You're taking up the entire hallway!'

Ella's heart jumped into her throat. She knew exactly who this was, rattling towards her. MISS JENKINS! THE GRANNYSAURUS REX FROM UPSTAIRS!

'Hello, Miss Jenkins,' Ella yelped. She was still pressed against the inside of the front door and definitely NOT taking up the entire hallway.

'HALL-HOG! How's a person supposed to get past with children in the way all the time? It's an outrage!' Miss Jenkins shrieked, kicking her slippered feet about as they dangled like socks on a washing line. 'I know who you are. You're that Griffin girl!' She hobbled out of her chair as it came to an abrupt stop above the bottom step, and started slowly shuffling towards Ella, brandishing her sticks like weapons. 'Don't think I won't clear you out the way with these!'

'I'm sorry, Miss Jenkins,' Ella said, trying to flatten herself against the wall and disappear. She was so panicked by the steadily approaching GRANNY-CERATOPS, she opened the front door wide and gestured for Miss Jenkins to head outside.

'I'm not in the mood for you, you little troublemaker.'

'It's nice to meet you too – and have a lovely day!' Ella cooed in pretend friendliness and, without thinking, glanced down onto the front step. 'Oh, bum,' she mumbled with a sinking feeling in her belly. Nula, Bertie and Violet were all staring up at her from the kerb. 'Um . . . er . . . morning!'

'I think we might need to start again,' Violet said. 'Y'know . . . with a proper hello.'

'Hi,' said Nula. 'It's nice to meet you – for real this time.'

They were all standing outside Minerva Mansions and Ella was experiencing a dizzying mixture of embarrassment and relief.

'I'm B-Bertie!' said Bertie, smiling and giving a little wave. 'You're Ella Gr-Gr-Griffin – we already know who you are.'

'Gossip travels quickly in Cod's Bottom,' Violet said.

'I'm not friends with her,' Ella blurted. She just had

to get the words out. 'I'm not friends with Veronica Ratsinger . . . in case you thought . . . I mean – I know you saw me with her, but I'm not . . .'

'We know,' Nula replied.

'She's horrib-b-ble about everyone,' said Bertie.

'And you don't seem mean enough to be her pampered pal,' added Nula with a laugh.

'Did she command you to be her new best friend?' Violet asked. 'She always does that . . . looking for the next person to boss about.'

'I was her best f-friend for about t-ten minutes before she realised I had a st-stammer,' Bertie said, crossing his arms.

'Her loss, Bertster.' Violet comforted him with a smile. 'You're brilliant.'

'That was a great idea, telling Veronica you had nits, Ella.' Nula snorted. 'I wish I'd thought of it. Everyone in town has been talking about how funny it was. At least, *we* have.'

Bertie nodded enthusiastically. 'Lots!' he said.

Ella smiled and looked at the three children nervously. She knew they'd have to talk about what happened the other day, but she wasn't sure where to even begin.

'I'm really sorry I yelled at you, Ella,' said Violet, breaking the moment of silence. 'Back at the Hippodrome I mean. I didn't know who it was, standing in the dark.'

86

'I can't believe I pushed you,' Ella replied. 'I don't know what I was thinking.'

'Oh, don't worry about that!' Nula laughed. She gave the pixie-haired girl a playful shove. 'Violet's fine! My head is way more important. It was spinning for hours after you bonce-butted me. You can run fast!'

Ella winced. 'Oh no! I'm sorry about that too. I must have really hurt you.'

'Doesn't matter,' Nula said with a shrug. She took Ella's hand and they all started walking downhill towards the harbour. 'Sorry you got the scare of your life.'

'There,' said Bertie, joining in. 'Ev-ev-everyone's sorry. We're all VERY s-sorry. Now can we go t-to the theatre?'

Ella felt her spine stiffen. 'We can't!' she gasped. 'I have to post a letter for my mum. And I . . . well, um . . .'

'We can p-post it on the way!' Bertie cheered. 'Let's go!'

'But what if we run into Veronica?' Ella asked, racking her brains for reasons not to go with them to the Hippodrome.

Nula laughed. 'We won't!'

'How do you know?' said Ella, feeling her knees starting to tremble.

'There was a mysterious nit scare, remember? It came out of nowhere!' Violet snorted with a grin. 'Ratsinger called a council meeting and everything.'

'Veronica called a council meeting? Can she do that?'

'Not her,' said Nula. 'We're talking about Veronica's dad – BIG RATSINGER!'

'RATZILLA!' Violet roared.

'Veronica's ratty dad went b-b-berserk after she locked herself in the loo and w-wouldn't come out,' Bertie said, practically twitching with glee. 'Ratzilla or-ordered everyone in town to use n-nit shampoo, or else!'

'Because of what I said?' Ella's mouth dropped open.

'You're a hero!' Nula whooped, swinging Ella's hand back and forth.

'And th-that's all that matters,' Bertie added. 'We all agree!'

'You mean I hid from you for two-and-a-bit days and I didn't need to?'

'Ha! You could have been out playing with us,' said Violet.

'But Ratzilla knows it was you who started the nit drama. Veronica squealed on you, just like she always does. I'm sure he'll be complaining to your mum soon enough,' Nula said as Ella's face creased with nervousness. 'Oh, don't worry. Ratzilla's not nearly as scary as Princess Prissy Poo-Poo-Plaits.'

'Who cares about Veronica's moany dad?' Violet hooted again. 'Ella is the defeater of all misery guts everywhere!' She stood to attention like the guards at Buckingham Palace. 'You're a hero and we all salute you!'

'So, can we go to the th-theatre now?' Bertie pleaded. 'I r-really want to show Ella around.'

Ella stopped in her tracks at the bottom of Cuttlebone Lane and felt her face turn the colour of Mrs Clott's smudgy lipstick. 'I need to ask a question first.'

Nula, Bertie and Violet all gave Ella the same knowing look.

'Yes!' Nula answered before Ella could get another word out. 'It's true.'

'What?' Ella said, bewildered.

'You did!' Violet agreed. 'Definitely.'

Ella felt even more confused. She didn't know whether to laugh or run back home. 'No . . . I mean . . . I don't think you—'

'We do!' Nula interrupted. 'We KNOW what you're going to ask, and you really did see what you think you saw.'

'You're NOT going crazy,' said Violet.

'They're our f-friends!' Bertie beamed, swishing his red cape. 'We've b-been visiting them since we w-were six!'

Ella tingled all over and curled her toes tightly. These children were just playing around . . . weren't they?

'Would you like to meet them?' asked Nula.

There was a long moment when nobody spoke. A seagull whirled overhead and its lonely cry made Ella shiver for the squillionth time that morning.

'They'd like t-to meet you,' Bertie said, breaking the not-quite-silence. 'We kn-know they would. They're super-n-nosy.'

Ella's knees felt like they were about to buckle and a lump popped into her throat. She opened her mouth but couldn't find any words to use, so, with a fluttering heart and trembling fingers, Ella simply nodded.

10
GHOSTS

Ella held her breath as she followed Nula, Violet and Bertie through the peeling doors and past the ticket office, their footsteps echoing off the dusty marble floors. This time around, she couldn't shake the feeling that *everything* was watching her – wherever she looked, the carved cherubs seemed to be shifting their gaze and gawking at them.

'It's n-not as sc-scary as you think,' Bertie said, trying to calm Ella's obvious jitters. 'I pr-promise.'

'Ha! You cried every time we came here for the first year, Bertster,' Nula snorted. 'We lost count of how many times you wet your pants!'

'I C-CAN'T HELP IT!' Bertie yelled. 'My nan says I'm a sensitive s-soul!'

'And we wouldn't change you,' Violet laughed sweetly in Bertie's ear as she crept up behind and made him jump. 'Not one bit.'

'Except for your  smelly feet,' Nula teased. 'Pong-o-riffic!'

'Hey!' Bertie folded his arms and pretended to be cross. 'I d-d-don't have smelly f-feet . . . all the time.'

The four children crossed the grand atrium, beneath the giant pigeon-crowded chandelier, and under a large arch behind the staircase that Ella hadn't spotted the last time. Her skin prickled at the thought of what unknown horrors might be waiting beyond it.

'It's not far now,' Violet whispered, giving Ella's hand a friendly squeeze. 'I bet they're all asleep. They'll be so surprised to wake up and meet you. Ghosts are so lazy in the daytime.'

Ella shivered. It was the first time she'd heard any of her new friends use the G word! She wanted to believe Violet, but something in her brain just couldn't let her do it. Even though she'd seen the floating ballerina and a gaggle of not-quite-there people, there had to be a simpler explanation than gho . . . than that.

A short hallway
lined with show posters stretched ahead of them as they
all passed beneath the arch. Ella read the faded lettering
with unexpected glee as she shuffled past, making her
forget her nervousness in a flash.

Each framed poster was stuffed full of sensational
pictures and lists of all the strange and wonderful variety
acts who'd performed at the Hippodrome years ago.
There were jugglers and stilt-walkers, trapeze artists,
singers, comedians, dance duos and orchestras. Some of
the posters were over a hundred years old!

'These are TERRIFIC!' she cried. '"Philomena
Flummery and her Prancing Poodles"!' Ella read aloud.
Hadn't Mum mentioned a poodle lady? Could this
be the one Sylvie used to talk about? '"The Toast of
London – Actor Octavius P. Gulch"! "Madame Eudora
Grebble, Psychic Extraordinaire"! And I wonder who
"The Great Stupendi" was?'

Violet smiled in the gloom and raised her eyebrows
playfully. 'They're all here, you know! You can find out
for yourself. This way . . .'

Ella gulped and felt her skin prickle. She followed the three children through another door and found herself in the lower level of the dark auditorium. She looked up to the balconies, searching for the spot where she'd been three days ago – where she'd got the fright of her life.

'H-here we are!' Bertie whooped. In the quiet stillness his voice suddenly seemed extremely loud. 'It's p-pretty, isn't it?'

Ella glanced about, investigating the shadows for spooks. The Hippodrome was definitely impressive, but she wasn't sure she'd call it 'pretty'. Everything was covered in cobwebs, pigeon feathers and mould. She wandered along one of the rows of tattered seats in the centre of the vast room. All was deathly still. The only movement Ella could see were swirls of dust that danced in and out of the shaft of daylight from the broken roof.

'What now?' she whispered.

'Now we wake them up,' Nula said. She headed over to Ella and placed a hand on her shoulder. 'You want to give it a try?'

'Um . . . all right,' Ella replied, suddenly feeling extremely self-conscious. What on earth was she supposed to say to a bunch of sleeping ghosts? She turned to face the stage and prayed that Nula, Violet and Bertie weren't just making fun of her.

'Hello?' Ella called in a feeble voice. This felt like the most ridiculous thing she'd ever done. 'Are you there? Anyone? Wake up!' She paused and listened for signs of rising wraiths or moaning manifestations. 'I don't think they can hear me,' Ella whispered. 'Maybe they're shy.'

'Theatre ghosts are a lot of things,' said Violet, 'but they're never shy.'

Bertie chuckled. 'That's n-not how you wake th-theatre ghosts,' he said, tripping along another row of seats a little closer to the stage. 'Can I d-do it?'

'You always want to do it,' Nula said, rolling her eyes.

'Please!' Bertie leaped from the end of his row and galloped up the aisle towards them. 'I'm re-really good at it. P-PLEASE!'

'Go on, then,' Nula said. 'But make it a good one.'

'I b-bet I can wake everyone up at once!' Bertie wedged his fists on his hips and struck a superhero pose. 'W-watch this, Ella!'

Ella's eyes were the size of teacups. This was it. This was actually the moment she was going to properly meet theatre ghosts. She watched as Bertie clambered up to stand on one of the seats. He cupped his hands round his mouth like a megaphone, and yelled: 'OH, LOOK! H-HERE'S SOMEONE N-NEW TO ENTERTAIN –' he turned to point at Ella – 'AND SHE'S NEVER B-B-BEEN TO A THEATRE

95

BEFORE! SHE N-NEEDS A GOOD OL' SONG-AND-DANCE SH-SHOW!'

'Hurrah! Be still my un-beating heart!' a voice cheered out of nowhere. It sounded echoey and distant, like someone shouting from the next room. 'How marvellous! A new audience member!'

There was a sudden explosion of clear glistening slime over the rows of seats and then . . . Ella nearly screamed and fainted all at the same time.

Flickering into view like someone striking a match in the darkness, a man appeared and floated in the air above the children's heads. Only he wasn't a man at all. The cherubs on the proscenium arch were visible through his tall, thin body, and he was giving off a pale greenish-blue glow, just like the stickers of stars and moons Ella used to have on her bedroom ceiling back in London.

'Where? WHERE is this new fellow?' the man asked frantically. He was wearing an old-fashioned bedcap and a long, ragged nightgown, and was sporting the curliest moustache Ella had ever seen. He turned to Bertie and flung his arms wide. 'I have some wondrous poetry that simply must be heard, Bertie my boy! Does this new audience member enjoy ballads? A spot of light *commedia* perhaps?'

'Oh, lummy! Did I hear there's someone who needs entertainin'?' another voice exclaimed. There was a second explosion of ghostly goop as a woman appeared above the aisle, only a tiny distance away from Ella and her new friends.

'Ugh! Watch out, Philomena!' Nula grumbled as the slime rained on them in a fine mist that smelled of lavender perfume.

Violet looked at Ella and smirked as she brushed some of the stuff off her elbow. 'Ectoplasm – you get used to it.'

Ella shuddered as the twinkling droplets landed on her arms, then evaporated instantly into nothing but smoke.

'Oh, I do beg your pardon,' the ghost named Philomena gasped as she spotted the four children below her. 'We wasn't expectin' company, not at this early hour. Caught me right on the hop, you did!'

Ella gawped at the see-through woman floating above her and marvelled. What an incredible thing to behold! Her glowing hair was clipped and curled in beautiful waves across the top of her head then it puffed out on either side of her neck like baubles. Beads and feathers covered the top of her curvy dress, and the bottom was a mass of candyfloss lace.

'I've been runnin' about all morning after those blasted poodles. They've been terrorising poor Mr Stupendi again, they have!'

'Not now, Philomena!' the phantom man snapped as he flew to the floor. 'There's someone in need of my dramatic stories. They certainly don't want to hear about your—'

'Oh, THERE she is!' Philomena cooed, interrupting her fellow ghost. She glided gently down to the tattered carpet and fixed Ella with her dazzling blue-green stare. 'And who might you be then, littl'un? I think we spotted you running away from here like you'd seen a ghost the other day. HA HA! GET IT?'

'This is Ella Gr-Griffin,' Bertie said, brimming with pride. 'Sh-she's n-new in town.'

'How bloomin' marvellous, Bertie,' Philomena said, leaning in to get a good look at Ella. 'It's very nice to meet you, dearie. You ain't seen any poodles runnin' about the place, 'ave you?'

Ella shook her head, not daring to answer. If she opened her mouth now, she might dribble down the front of her dungarees. A real-life ghost . . . or rather a REAL-DEAD ghost was actually speaking to her! Suddenly the whole world seemed wonky and wild.

'What have your pooches been up to, Philly?' Violet asked, laughing. 'Where are they?'

'They're a rotten nuisance,' moaned the tall man, giving Philomena a disgusted look. 'Just follow your nose if you want to find them. Who knew haunted hounds could still stink of wet fur and gutter muck?'

'You watch your tongue, Gulch! My poodles smell beau'iful!' Philomena shot the other ghost a scowl, before turning back to Ella. 'Don't worry about him, darlin'. He's a right grumpy ol' ghoul at the best of times.'

'Such rudeness, Philomena!' The man drifted to the centre of the aisle and took a small bow. 'Allow me to make the first grand introduction of all the spirits here, young lady. Nay, hold your applause! For I am the Toast of London, the Pride of Piccadilly, the Bard of Bermondsey, the Poet of Pimlico, the Lyricist of Leicester Square – ACTOR EXTRAORDINAIRE! I AM OCTAVIUS P. GULCH!'

'Your name ain't Octavius!' Philomena snickered.

'Shut up!' the man blustered back at her. 'Don't you dare, Philomena!'

'Your name is not fancy-flouncy "Octavius" Gulch!'

'Yes it is!'

'No it ain't!' Philomena guffawed. 'Never was, never will be!'

'It's my *stage* name. All professional thespians use one, I'll have you know, and I'd like to go by mine on this occasion—'

'His name . . .' Philomena turned to Ella with shimmering tears of laughter in her eyes. 'His name is—'

'You're despicable, Miss Flummery!'

'His name is . . . is . . . Morris!' Philomena fell about

laughing. 'Plain old Morris Gulch! Boring as dry toast!'

'Shame on you!' If it hadn't already been pale green, Ella could have sworn Morris's face was turning purple. 'Now you've spoiled my grand introduction, Philomena. The whole day is ruined!'

'Oh, you think *that's* bad? Just wait till you realise you're still in your jim-jams, Morris!' Philomena chortled.

A look of horror spread across Morris's face. He glanced down at his nightgown, croaked an odd sort of scream, then vanished in another explosion of ectoplasm.

'He'll be back,' said Violet, smiling at Ella. 'Five . . . four . . . three . . . two . . .'

SPLOOF! In the exact spot he'd been standing seconds before, Morris reappeared, looking slightly flustered, only this time he was dressed smartly in a silk shirt, velvet tailcoat and bowtie. There was a ridiculously tall top hat perched on his balding head and he prodded it about to make sure it was in exactly the right place. 'Much better! Where were we?' he finally said. 'Ah, yes! I shall start my grand introduction again—'

A-WOOOOOOOOO!

Ella dived for safety behind Nula and Violet as the howling of excited dogs echoed through the auditorium. She'd already seen two spooks this morning, but still wasn't prepared for what came next.

'Not again,' Morris grumbled. 'How undignified.'

Through the wall on the far side of the auditorium sprinted a . . . A PAIR OF GHOSTLY LEGS, with three yipping and yapping phantom poodles in hot pursuit, nipping at the ankles and trying to bite the ownerless backside.

A-WOOOOOOOOO!!

'Stop! Come back!'

Ella couldn't believe what she was seeing. As the disembodied legs and three spectral poodles sped along the back of the vast room and down the central aisle, another figure hurried through the wall, hollering and wailing. It was a male ghost, wearing a brightly coloured outfit. He looked like someone who might've belonged to an old circus, but he seemed to completely vanish below the waist.

'My legs! Come back, my legs!' the ghost bawled in a strong Italian accent.

It didn't take Ella very long to figure out the frenzied limbs, dressed in matching diamond-patterned pantaloons and pointed shoes with pom-poms at the ends, belonged to him.

'My legs! Wait for me, my *bellissime* legs!' he sobbed. 'Come to me, please STOP, *per favore!*'

'Oh, *there* you are, girlies!' Philomena cooed when she saw her poodles racing towards them, ignoring the legs altogether. 'That's enough playtime, my pets.' Raising her fingers to her lips, Philomena let rip a shrill, ear-jangling whistle and the three dogs suddenly gave up their chase and skidded to a halt.

Ella had been watching it all in delight. 'WOW!' she hooted. This was shaping up to be the most thrilling day of her life.

'Come back! Oh, my ankles! My knees!' the circus ghost pleaded from the back of the theatre, but his legs continued running. They darted straight through Bertie's body like smoke and dived into the front boards of the stage, melting from view. '*Arrivederci*, my dancing feet!' he called, sadly.

Philomena clapped her hands. 'Show time, girlies!' she commanded, drawing all attention back to her amazing poodles. In perfect unison, the three dogs sprang into the air, somersaulted, then landed one on top of the other in a fluffy tower next to their owner. They wobbled on the spot and panted happily as they glowed turquoise in the gloom.

'That was brilliant!' Ella blurted. She looked at Bertie. His jeans, T-shirt and cape were now twinkling with ectoplasm after the legs had made their escape right through him.

'It's f-funny when they do that,' he giggled, brushing himself down. 'Ooh, it's all cold and tingly!'

'Well, Ella, it looks like I'll 'ave the pleasure of the first uninterrupted introduction, after all,' Philomena said, shooting Morris an amused glance. 'I'm Philomena Flummery and these are my Prancing Poodles – Allegra, Electra and Olympia!'

As their names were called, each ghostly dog tumbled from the pooch-tower and landed on its front paws, performing a handstand.

'BRAVO!' Ella couldn't help applauding the spectacular creatures. 'It's SO nice to meet you, Philomena! My dog, Wilson, could never do that.'

'Oh, we ain't even started!' The ghost lady gave another sharp whistle and her three pets did forward rolls into perfect sitting positions. 'Wotcha think, Ella?'

'I think they're fantastic!' Ella exclaimed. Before she could stop herself, she reached out to pat the nearest

poodle on top of its fluffy head—

'AGH!' Ella recoiled in shock and embarrassment as her hand sank right into the middle of Olympia's snout. 'Oh, I'm sorry!'

'Ha! Don't you go worryin' about that,' Philomena chuckled. 'Happens all the time.'

Ella examined her fingers and felt a quiver of wonder as they sparkled for a second. She turned to Olympia, who was cheerfully wagging her puffball tail, and then squealed with joy when the dog stuck a phantom tongue straight through her palm.

'It's all frosty!' Ella yelped. 'It feels like ice crystals fizzing under my skin!'

'I t-told you it was funny,' Bertie said. 'It's like b-bubbles in the bath and popping c-candy.'

'That's all well and good,' Morris grumbled, his bottom lip trembling, 'but we can't stand around here all day crowing at clowning canines. Perhaps our new guest would like to see something a little more highbrow?'

'Umm . . . I'd like that very much,' said Ella. The last thing she wanted was to upset one of the theatre ghosts on her first visit. 'I love plays . . . and poems!'

'Music to my ears!' Morris looked like he was about to swoon with joy. 'I knew it! I knew as soon as I saw you, dear girl. I said to myself, "Now, there's a person of fine intelligence!"'

The tall ghost flew into the air and headed for the stage, landing again in the shaft of light. He stood as straight and as tall as he could, corrected the positioning of his over-sized top hat, and took a deep breath. 'I shall start with a little Shakespeare!' he declared, striking a pose, with one finger pressed against his furrowed brow. '"When forty winters shall—"'

'Giuseppe!' Philomena suddenly cooed, sending her poodles into fits of barking and yapping. 'Nice of you to join us!'

Ella turned round and jumped with fright. Right behind her floated the miserable-looking half-man in his clown make-up and fancy circus outfit.

'BOTHER AND BLAST, GIUSEPPE!' Morris moaned from the stage. He stamped his foot angrily ... or he would have stamped it angrily if it hadn't disappeared straight into the floor. 'I HADN'T FINISHED!'

'Oh, ignore him, Giuseppe,' Philomena told the unhappy latecomer. 'Why don't you introduce yourself to our guest?'

'*Ciao, bella signorina*,' the half-ghost whimpered, pulling a face like he was about to burst into tears. 'I am . . .'

'You can do it, dearie,' Philomena reassured him. She pointed at Ella. 'Us show folk are nuffin' without a good introduction, and we've got a new friend to entertain.'

'I am the . . .' It was barely a squeak – more of a despondent snivel than an introduction, really. Giuseppe attempted to present his arms in the air, but they were bent and droopy at the elbow. 'I am . . .'

'Keep going, Giuseppe,' Violet joined in. 'I know you can.'

The ghost nodded, looking sadder than a dropped omelette.

'I am the Great Stupendi!' he blubbed. 'The top half of him anyway . . .'

'The best half,' Nula said with a sincere nod.

'Oh dear,' said Ella, trying to comfort the dejected ghost. She reached out to put her hand on his shoulder, but quickly remembered Olympia the poodle and stopped herself. 'What happened?'

'It's a very *LOOOOONNNNNGGGG* story, Ella,' Philomena commented, winking at her and shaking her head as if to say, *Don't ask!*

'Giuseppe has been chasing his legs for nearly two hundred years, haven't you?' Nula said.

'I have!' he cried. 'And I'm so tired!'

'Poor Giuseppe!' Bertie sighed. 'Th-the chase hasn't g-gone well.'

'They got away in a magic accident,' Nula continued.

'That's right,' Giuseppe agreed. 'Such fast legs. *Arrivederci!*'

108

'His assistant was late the night of their big performance here,' Violet whispered in Ella's ear, 'so Giuseppe decided to do a solo magic show without her. He tried to cut *himself* in half, instead of her, and well . . . It didn't quite go as planned.'

Ella winced at Violet, and Violet shrugged back, sticking out her tongue like she was going to be sick.

Mr Stupendi sniffed. 'I will tell you the full story. You sit comfortably, yes?'

'Wait a minute – why does Stupendi get to tell his ridiculous story and I am denied my Shakespearian spectacular!?' Morris suddenly ranted from the stage. 'I swear I should never have come to this wretched town and its pokey little theatre. I'm surrounded by AMATEURS. I was the star of Drury Lane, don't you know? Hailed as a true master by Queen Victoria herself! I should be haunting one of London's great show palaces. Instead, I wind up popping my clogs *here* – after one performance with no one to appreciate my art!'

'Don't start!' groaned Philomena. 'None of us could help where or how we went, Morris. You know that! And we can't all entertain Ella at once, can we?'

SPLOOF!

As if in answer to Philomena's words, ANOTHER small explosion of ectoplasm interrupted the conversation.

This one smelled of incense and burning herbs, and the glowing ghost of a tiny woman sparkled into view.

Ella, who was pretty certain she'd had more than enough shocks for one day, stumbled back in surprise.

'Oh, *just* what we need!' Morris complained, and turned his back on everyone. 'More *rabble*. What's that cantankerous old goat crawled out of the cracks for this time?'

The bent-over woman was a mass of petticoats and shawls. She had rings on every finger and bracelets all the way up both arms. On her head sat a clump of knotted scarves, wrapped and twisted and stuck-about with pins and trinkets, and a brooch in the shape of an open eye was fastened right above the centre of her forehead.

'I am Madame—' Unfortunately, the ancient granny-ghost coughed before she could finish her first sentence and a crumbling set of phantom dentures flew out of her puckered mouth and floated off towards the ceiling.

'Ha ha!' Bertie burst out laughing, but Nula quickly shushed him.

'Oh, bother,' the old woman now rasped between toothless gums, spraying her audience with ectoplasmic spit. 'I sensed that was going to happen.'

'Shall we try that again?' said Philomena encouragingly. She signalled to her poodles and they instantly raced into the air and fetched the rogue set of chompers, returning them in a flash. 'There you go, dearie.' Philomena handed the dentures back to the elderly spook and she popped them in her mouth, smacking her lips a few times to make sure they were secure.

'I am Madame Grebble!' she declared, peering at Ella over little round glasses and twitching her wiry eyebrows. 'Psychic! Mystic! Seer of the Seven Spirit Realms! I sense . . . UGH! Something is coming through! It's on its way . . . yes, I can see it now . . .'

Everyone quietly watched as Madame Grebble started gyrating on the spot, grunting and snorting.

'I sense . . . I sense . . .' She jabbed a gnarled finger in Ella's face. 'Your name is Ronald!'

'Bravo!' Morris jeered sarcastically from the stage, slowly clapping his hands.

'Um, no, not quite – it's Ella!' said Ella. She wasn't sure if the wild-eyed woman had been joking.

'Yes! Ella! That's right – I sensed it. ELLA!' Madame Grebble corrected herself with a wheeze. 'Your name is ELLA! Do I speak true?'

'Er, yes . . .' Ella said, trying not to giggle as the fortune teller skipped from stumpy foot to stumpy foot in her psychic trance.

'I knew it! My powers are stronger than ever!' Madame Grebble started hopping like she was trying to take off. 'And I sense—'

'BOG OFF, GREBBLE!' Morris heckled.

'I sense . . .' Madame Grebble folded her arms triumphantly. 'I sense you're a little bit startled this morning.'

12
THE DAILY LIVES OF THE DEAD

As the morning faded into the afternoon, more and more of the theatre's haunted inhabitants gathered in the vast auditorium to ogle and gossip about the new human in their midst, and Ella ogled them right back. She'd already met Madame Grebble's enormous cat, Lakshmi; been serenaded by a spectral band of musicians who floated out of the orchestra pit; and now was being offered a suspiciously seawater-tasting cup of tea by an invisible . . . something.

'Thanks, Pendle!' Violet said to the empty air as she took hold of her floating teacup.

'P-Pendle is the theatre's p-poltergeist,' Bertie explained. 'No one can see or hear him . . . her . . . th-them. No one can see or hear them.'

Nula beamed into the dusty gloom. 'Lovely cup of tea, Pendle!' She pretended to sip it, then turned to Ella and mouthed, 'Don't drink it,' before carefully pouring the contents of her cup into the motheaten carpet. 'Mmm, delicious!'

The four children and their phantom friends had recently been joined by a muscly strongman, who had drifted up through the floor. Alonzo McBurnie in his leopard-print leotard was sitting close by in mid-air, busy knitting a scarf and showering balls of wafty wood in all directions.

'It's been so long since I've seen one of you skin-and-boney-types,' said Alonzo. 'I feel chuffed enough to blub.'

Nula snorted. 'What are you talking about, Alonzo? Me, Bertie, and Violet visit all the time!'

'I know, I know,' Alonzo said. 'But it's been ages since we've seen anyone *new* of the fleshy variety.' He flexed his massive bicep and looked at it thoughtfully. 'I miss having skin and bones. What I wouldn't give to be able to hug someone – or feel a few aches and pains now and again.'

'How is dear, darling London?' Morris asked over the chitter-chatter. He'd finally given up on his sulking and come to float nearby with a look of fascination on his face. 'Is she still a city of astounding beauty? There must be so many theatres named after me by now. How I wish I could haunt them all!'

'I bet London is full of mechanical gentlemen with

good manners these days,' mused a stout ghost named Clementine Cramps from a little way off. Ella hadn't seen her before and gasped. She was absent-mindedly swishing her enormous ballgown around and twiddling a beard that sprouted from her chin in great twisted tufts. 'There'll be steam-powered flying shops selling corsets that actually lace themselves up, I'm sure . . .'

'Well, not really,' Ella replied to Clementine, trying not to stare. She'd never seen a bearded lady before. How was she going to keep up and remember everyone's name? She'd have pages and pages of lists to write after this. 'The shops don't fly – they're still on the ground – and ladies don't wear corsets any more.'

'Don't wear corsets!?!?' Clementine gasped. Her wispy whiskers bristled and curled. 'Why, ladies must be walking around practically NAKED!'

'No.' Ella smirked. 'Not exactly.'

'I sensed that,' Madame Grabble rasped with a sly grin and a nod. 'I sensed the shops were still on the ground. It's my talent.'

'INCOMING!'

Ella turned round just in time to see two ghostly girls swoop across the auditorium on a glowing trapeze. They soared above the rows of seats, then vaulted through the air and landed gracefully among the gathered crowd without making a sound.

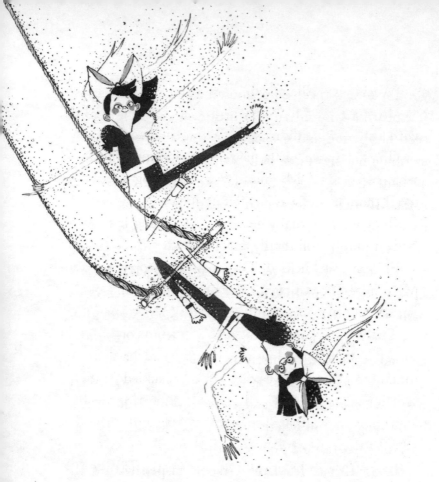

'The cobwebs are whispering,' said the first girl.

'They say a stranger is here,' said the other. The pair were identical with their neatly bobbed hair and enormous ribbon bows. 'Is it another one of those blasted workmen?'

'No, don't fret, dearies,' Philomena soothed. 'We've had no workmen today.'

'Workmen?' Ella asked.

'They're going to demolish the theatre,' said Nula, with a shrug. She didn't seem too worried about it.

'That's terrible!' Ella gasped, wondering why Nula seemed so calm. 'My mum said something about that too. I thought she was just telling fibs.'

'They won't actually get around to doing it though,' Nula went on, still totally unconcerned.

Philomena chuckled. 'Oh, don't you worry yourself, Miss Ella. They've been saying it for years and yonks, but no one ever does a thing about it.'

'Every now and then, the Cod's Bottom council send some blunderin' bawlow in a hard hat to have a look round the place, but we scare 'em off,' cackled Madame Grebble. Her laugh was like a gurgling drain. 'They won't ever knock the place down. Pendle will throw 'em all out before they try, won't you, ducky?'

In answer to Madame Grebble's question, a clump of dust and old leaves plucked itself from the carpet, flew into the air and spelled the word **YES!**

'So, what's happening?' the two acrobatic twins went on.

'We b-brought our new friend!' Bertie answered gleefully, gesturing in Ella's direction. 'Ella Griffin. She j-just moved to Cod's Bot-to-tom.'

The girls fixed Ella with their unblinking stare.

117

'Hello,' Ella said, giving a timid smile. 'It's nice to meet you.'

'Someone new!' the girls exclaimed together.

'I'm Florrie Tunk,' said one.

'I'm Vesta Tunk,' said the other.

'We're the Tunk Twins,' they said in perfect unison, eyeing Ella curiously. 'What do you do?'

'Yes,' Clementine Cramps joined in. 'What *do* you do, child?'

'Do? I . . . I don't understand,' Ella replied.

'It's a simple question,' the twins said blankly.

'Um . . .' Ella suddenly felt very shy. All these staring eyes were starting to make her want to hide behind the nearest grimy pillar.

'What do you DO?' asked Florrie. 'Everyone has a talent.'

'We ride the wind,' said Vesta.

'On the flying trapeze,' they said together.

'Oh . . . er . . .' Ella's thoughts raced and she could feel herself blushing. 'I think I'm quite good at acting. I go to a Saturday drama club. Well, I used to, I mean. And I've been thinking about ballet quite a bit recently—'

'Excellent!' Morris beamed. 'Most excellent!'

'I c-can do *this*!' Bertie chimed in. He swung his arm round in a circle, then smiled and took a bow.

'I talk to ghosts!' Madame Grebble croaked as she

stood up, sending Lakshmi tumbling off her lap with an angry *MEOW!* The haggard mystic wriggled her bejewelled fingers again and peered over her spectacles, trying to look as mysterious as possible. 'I can hear the whisperings of the dead!'

'So what, you juddery fraud?' Morris scoffed. 'We can all do that!'

'Shut your sauce-box, Morris!' Madame Grebble placed two fingers against each temple. 'I sense you're about three seconds away from getting booted in your big boring backside.'

'Calm yourself, Eudora,' Philomena warned.

'He started it!' Madame Grebble squawked back, crinkling her flustered face into a scowl. 'I *sense* he's a dung-brained flapdoodle!'

'How dare you!' Morris looked outraged. He quickly turned away and began fussing over his wonky top hat to hide his mortification.

'Oh yes, back to your sulking you go,' Grebble hooted.

'Enough, you two!' Philomena shouted over the hubbub. 'Nula, Bertie and Violet 'ave brought their lovely little friend to see us, and she don't want to listen to all this gripin'!'

All eyes settled back on Ella like they were expecting her to say something, and Ella didn't know what to do. She looked from each phantom face to the next and felt an overwhelming urge to grab her trusty green notebook and start a new list right then and there. That would calm her nerves for certain, but she had more questions she wanted to ask first.

'Um . . . I hope you don't mind me asking, but is this all of you?' With the mention of talent and ballet, Ella's mind had drifted back to the ballerina. 'Only, I saw a dancer before and I'd love to meet her properly.'

'Oh, there's loads more of us, darlin',' said Philomena, 'wandering the nooks and haunting the crannies. You'll meet all the spooks eventually, I'm sure. This place is busier than Charing Cross Station some days! You're talking about Giselle. The ballerina, I mean. She haunts the quiet corners and just stares out of windows mostly – although you won't get much gossip out of her. She's not exactly a talker. Come to think of it, I don't think I've ever heard her speak.'

'I'd love to try and talk with her,' said Ella. 'I saw her here on stage – and in my bedroom.'

'In your bedroom?' Madame Grebble scoffed. 'What nonsense!'

'She was,' Ella said. 'I swear!'

'I think you might be a bit confused there, Miss Griffin,' said Morris, joining in. 'You see, a ghost is tethered to its haunt. We're stuck in this mildewed mess of a place, so it would be quite impossible for

Giselle to visit your bedroom. We can barely get as far as the gate before we're dragged back inside by invisible strings. It's like being a wretched puppet!'

'Oh . . .' Ella felt confused. There was no way she'd imagined the ballerina in her bedroom. She'd seen Giselle with her own eyes! But Ella didn't want to argue with Madame Grebble and Morris, so she left it at that, determined to find the graceful ghost and ask her herself.

'Anyhoo,' Philomena went on, more cheerfully, 'you're 'ere with the rest of us now, Ella, and we've been itching to put on a show for a month of gloomy Mondays. What do you say? Who would you like to see on stage? Which of our acts tickle your fancy?'

Ella thought for a moment. Then, with butterflies in her stomach and tingles in her toes, she declared: 'All of you! I want to see EVERYONE perform!'

When five o'clock arrived, Ella practically floated back to Minerva Mansions like one of the glorious ghosts she'd spent the day with. Having waved goodbye to Nula, Bertie and Violet as they passed their houses on the way home, Ella could hardly stop herself skipping, twirling and singing to herself as she made her way up Cuttlebone Lane. What a day! Everything seemed to sparkle with a new glint of magic – no, a glint of *ectoplasm*! – just knowing there were really-real ghosts in the local theatre! In one day alone, she'd made lots of new friends, living *and* dead, and Ella was twitching with happiness. To think she'd been hiding in her room!

'There you are, darling! How was your day? Did you do anything exciting?'

Ella found Mum cooking at the kitchen stove and she gulped, suddenly realising she hadn't planned what to say when she got home.

'Er, brill . . .' was all she managed. 'Today was . . . amazing.'

'You promise?' Mum said with a concerned face. 'I thought I heard you wailing and gnashing when you were coming up the stairs. It sounded like you were crying.'

'Mum!' Ella half gasped, half laughed. 'I was *singing* to myself!'

'Oh, um . . .' Mum pulled a face and tried not to smirk. 'I knew that. It sounded . . . lovely.'

Ella frowned, but couldn't stop herself from giggling. 'I've made some new friends. Great ones – a bit like Ava and Yusif.'

'Oh, sweetheart, that makes me so happy,' Mum gushed, rushing over to hug her daughter. 'I was a little bit worried about you yesterday.'

'I'll be fine now.' Ella squeezed Mum tightly. 'What's for dinner? I'm starving!'

The rest of the evening passed in a cheerful blur. After mugs of pea-and-ham soup with crusty bread, Ella dashed back to her brilliant new bedroom. She was so happy as she leaped on her bed she didn't even mind when Miss Jenkins started shrieking at her telly upstairs ('I'M SICK OF COOKING PROGRAMMES!').

Ella snuggled up next to Wilson and grinned.

'Just another *normal* day in Cod's Bottom, eh, Wilsy?'

She spent the next few hours before bedtime doodling pictures of the ghosts she'd met, and writing lists of every detail she could remember about them.

Theatre Ghosts

Philomena Flummery - poodle lady

Allegra, Electra and Olympia - the Prancing Poodles

Morris Gulch - actor (aka Octavius P. Gulch)

Giuseppe - the Great Stupendi (or clowny-magician-person missing his legs)

Madame Eudora Grebble - psychic (she SENSES)

Lakshmi - Madame Grebble's cat (very big, very fluffy)

Clementine Cramps - bearded lady
Alonzo McBurnie - strongman
   (leotard and knitting)
Florrie and Vesta Tunk - trapeze
   artists
Pendle - theatre poltergeist
Giselle - ballerina (doesn't talk?)
Musicians - in the orchestra
Cherubs (NOSY!)

'I bet Madame Grebble and Morris are still arguing,' Ella thought out loud, staring through the window at the night sky. 'And I wonder if Mr Stupendi caught his legs? You'd love Philomena's poodles, Wilsy – and you'd definitely have a good bark at Lakshmi!'

13
UNWELCOME VISITORS

When the next day came, Ella was already dressed and down in the kitchen eating breakfast before Mum had even called her. She wolfed down her crumpets, grabbed her coat and raced down the stairs, passing Miss Jenkins rattling up the other way on her rickety stairlift.

'Hello, Evelyn!' Ella trilled, full of excitement. 'It's a lovely morning.'

'Is it?' the cantankerous lady grumbled as she rounded the corner of the banister. 'I'm not in the mood for any of it! AND IT'S MISS JENKINS TO YOU!'

Ella didn't reply. Nothing – absolutely NOTHING – could ruin the day for her, not even scary old Evelyn Jenkins. She yanked open the front door, whistling as she did so, dashed out into the grey morning light, and ran straight into a tall and very stern-looking man who was standing at the front step.

'Miss Griffin, I presume?' he snapped as Ella shuffled back, steadying herself. 'Am I addressing the correct person?'

Ella looked up at the scowling man. He was dressed in a drab grey suit the colour of washing-up water and his dark hair was scraped into crispy lines across a bald patch on the top of his head. She looked down, spotted her own worried reflection in his perfectly polished shoes and realised her morning might be ruined after all.

'That's her, Daddy!' A snivelling voice came from somewhere behind the grim stick of a man and Ella recognised it immediately. 'Teach her a lesson, the filthy BUG-BURGER!' It was Veronica, which meant Ella had just run head-first into BIG RATSINGER! RATZILLA!

'Tell her off, Daddy.' Veronica stepped into view, wearing a bright pink bobble hat with her plaits stuffed up underneath it. 'She's unusual!'

'Are you Miss Griffin?' Ratzilla asked again. He had the face of someone chewing on gristle. 'Miss Ella Griffin?

'Yes, Mr Ratsinger,' Ella said nervously.

'MISTER!?!' The thin moustache that drooped across Ratzilla's top lip twitched as he sneered at her. 'You will address me as "Councillor Ratsinger", young lady!'

'Oh . . . um . . . yes, sorry, Councillor Ratsinger.'

'Good. That's better.' Ratzilla stooped to get a better look at Ella with an expression of utter revulsion. 'I think we need to have a little *chat*.'

***

'I c-can't believe R-Ratzilla actually came to your house!' Bertie spluttered through a mouthful of popcorn.

'You should have slammed the door in his face,' Nula said as she passed round a bag of sweets with one hand and scooped up a fistful of popcorn with the other. 'I would have shoved 'em right off the doorstep. Who wants another sour gum? The green ones taste like lemon and lime.'

'I'm so full,' Violet groaned. She grabbed her jumper from the floor and stuffed it under her T-shirt. 'I'M GOING TO EXPLODE!'

'What are they like?' Clementine Cramps asked with wide, hungry eyes as she watched the children chewing. 'Sour gums, I mean . . . I can't remember flavours. What I wouldn't give to know the taste of a green sour gum. We only had bits of dried fruit when I was a young 'un.'

'Bleugh!' Nula retched. 'That's not a treat!'

'My old ma used to give us a lump of wood to gnaw on if we were good,' Madame Grebble said, shaking her head at the array of brightly coloured sweet wrappers strewn across the floor. 'We didn't have any of these gummy whatnots.'

Ella and her new friends, both living and dead, were sitting in the theatre's atrium on a raggedy old stage curtain that they'd stretched out like a picnic blanket, surrounded by snacks and bottles of pop that Bertie's nan had packed for him from her sweet shop.

'Councillor Ratsinger even made Mum come down to the front door,' Ella groaned as she continued her story.

'Did he still have that hideous grey suit on?' Violet asked. 'Why can't people like that ever wear anything colourful? Or smile? Or laugh?'

'Yep!' Ella went on. 'Ratzilla was hopping mad about the nits thing. I explained it was a false alarm, but he's insisting Veronica keeps a pink woolly hat on her head to protect her from stray fleas whenever she's in town.

She looked like a snivelling snowman!'

'Ha ha!' Philomena guffawed from her perch on the bottom step. 'You trickster, Ella. I wish I could have been there to see it. Those Ratsingers have been in Cod's Bottom, bullying and making a nuisance for generations. They were gripin' around all the way back when I was a living thing just like you.'

'My mum said the same thing,' said Ella.

'Go on – do your impression again!' Violet cooed between mouthfuls of chocolate biscuit. 'Ella showed us on the way here,' she told Philomena. 'It's hilarious!'

Ella gawped at Violet and instantly felt herself blushing. 'No!' she blurted. How could she perform in front of all her terrifically talented new friends? This was much scarier than Saturday drama club. What if they all booed?

'Oh, g-go on, Ella,' Bertie joined in. He turned to the ghosts dotted about on the tattered curtain. 'It's really good. I've seen it too.'

'I love a good impersonation,' Alonzo chuckled as he knitted. 'I was always terrible at them.'

'Yes, do show us, Miss Griffin,' Morris said with a nod. 'This dastardly character sounds intriguing.'

'I . . . I . . . well . . .' Ella mumbled, trying to think of an excuse. 'I haven't got a costume. I'd need a costume to do it properly.'

'Pendle can sort that out in a jiffy,' whooped Nula. She clambered to her feet, tossed the empty bag of sour gums over her shoulder and yelled into the air: 'Pendle! Ella needs a costume!'

For a tiny moment, nothing happened, and Ella felt a whoosh of relief that Pendle probably hadn't heard Nula. But when several motheaten suit jackets soared down into the foyer from one of the higher floors, she knew she was out of luck.

'There we go, dearie. Take your pick,' Madame Grebble said, grinning a gappy grin as she stroked Lakshmi on her lap. 'Go for it. We could all use a good giggle!'

Five minutes later, Ella found herself halfway up the staircase, wearing one of the tatty suit jackets and looking down at the upturned faces of her friends.

'Well,' she muttered, as moths fluttered around inside her belly. 'It went something like this . . .'

Ella contorted her face into an extreme sneer and made her voice as nasal as she could— '*MISS ELLA GRIFFIN, I PRESUME?*'

'Pah!' Bertie burst out laughing and spat a mouthful of popcorn straight through Giuseppe's head, but the ghost was too miserable about his missing legs to even notice.

'She's hardly started yet, Bertster!' Nula poked Bertie in his side and giggled. '*Shhh!*'

'*I think we need to have a little chat,*' Ella went on in her

130

Ratzilla voice, scowling and grimacing. *'I've been hearing some very worrying things around the town. Rumours! Horrifying tales about cleanliness and personal hygiene!'*

Philomena snorted. 'He he, that's a Ratsinger if ever I've seen one!' She laughed a great big belly laugh and her poodles threw back their heads and howled. 'They're all the same!'

'He kept squirting hand sanitiser into his palms,' Ella said in her own voice. She was starting to enjoy herself. 'I think he thought I was a headlouse myself.'

'Do more! Do more!' Nula barked.

Ella began to rub her hands together and sneered even harder, making the group titter.

'My little Veronica was inconsolable, Miss Griffin,' Ella continued in a whiney voice. *'Bringing an outbreak of headlice into Cod's Bottom is a very serious violation of the town rules. My rules! Here in the district of Upper Haddock Norton, we demand a much higher standard!'*

'What town rules?' Violet exclaimed. 'He thinks he's the mayor – no, the *king* of Cod's Bottom!'

'I bet he thinks girls are stupid!' Nula growled, crossing her arms and frowning. 'Well, he can think again!'

'That's when Mum came downstairs and they had a bit of a stand-off,' Ella explained to her captive audience. 'He was rude about my family, and Mum nearly knocked his block off. She was amazing!'

131

'What d-did he say?' Bertie asked.

'It turns out Ratsinger and my aunt didn't get on,' Ella said. 'Before she died, she led the big campaign to stop Ratzilla from shutting down Cod's Bottom Library and selling off the land.'

'Your aunt sounds like a marvellous woman,' Morris cooed and clapped his hands.

'She was,' Ella said, beaming with pride. 'Sylvie Griffin, my mum's sister. I miss her very much.'

'OH MY LAWD!' Philomena practically rocketed into the air as her poodles yipped and barked. 'SYLVIE GRIFFIN?'

'Yes,' Ella replied.

'*Our* little Sylvie Griffin?'

Ella suddenly remembered what Mum had told her about Aunt Sylvie. How could she have let it slip her mind?

'Sorry, I forgot!' Ella blurted. 'Mum told me that, when they were girls, Sylvie used to talk about a poodle lady.'

'That was ME!' Philomena blubbed.

'Ella, do you mean to tell us that you are dear Sylvie's niece?' Morris asked. He flourished a haunted handkerchief from his top pocket and handed it to Philomena.

'That's right,' said Ella as a million questions flooded her head. Maybe these ghosts could tell her things about

Aunt Sylvie that even Mum couldn't.

'Little Sylvie,' Philomena gasped between sobs. 'I loved that girl. She used to sneak into the Hippodrome, and we'd spend hours laughing and playing. Oh, it was years ago!'

Nula, Bertie and Violet looked at Ella like she'd just turned into a dinosaur.

'Hang on,' Nula grunted. 'You mean we're *not* the first kids to visit you?'

'No! There have been lots through the years, my ducklings,' said Madame Grebble.

'There was Maisie Markham back in 1927,' Alonzo mused. 'She used to knit with me out on the veranda. Lovely child.'

'Bobby Griswald,' said Florrie Tunk.

'And Penelope Griswald,' said Vesta.

'Twins from 1952,' they both said together.

'I liked Graham,' Clementine sighed. 'Such a pretty face and feathers . . .'

Morris turned slowly to the bearded lady and rolled his eyes. 'Graham was a pigeon!'

'I know!' Clementine shot back. 'That doesn't mean he didn't have a pretty face!'

'But I thought we were special,' Nula replied flatly as the ghosts started to squabble.

'You are, darlin'!' said Philomena over the din. 'Our

afterlife would be nothing but Morris's grumbling and Giuseppe's wailing after his legs if we didn't have you lot.'

'No offence taken,' Morris scoffed.

'But who'd have guessed that one of those littl'uns from the past would have a niece who also comes to visit us years and years later?' Philomena went on. She turned to Ella and smiled kindly. 'That's warmed my frosty heart, that has.'

'I wish she was still around, Philly. Why isn't Sylvie a ghost too?' Ella asked.

Philomena shrugged. 'I supposed she didn't have any unfinished business,' she said. 'Not everyone becomes a ghost, you know – only the restless, wriggly ones.'

Ella nodded and tried to take it all in. She missed Aunt Sylvie more than ever and wished they could have visited the Hippodrome together.

'Mum said Sylvie used to talk about Giselle the ballerina too,' Ella said. 'That's why I'd like to see her again. I think she was trying to give me a message when she appeared in my room.'

'Giselle wasn't in your room, Ella!' Violet chuckled. 'You must have been dreaming. No ghost can leave their haunt, remember?'

'Violet's right,' Alonzo agreed. 'Believe me, I've tried. It's so frustrating knowing there's a wool shop just on the promenade – owned by an ancestor of Maisie

Markham, I've heard . . . All those yarns, just out of reach. Oh, the things I'd knit!'

'Well, I'd still like to find her and ask,' Ella said.

'Don't you worry, Miss Griffin,' said Morris reassuringly. 'Giselle's around here somewhere – you'll find her eventually. But for now, who's for a spot of poetry?'

'Not on your nelly!' Philomena shrieked and, in response to another of her high-pitched whistles, her three poodles chased the complaining ghost across the atrium and through the nearest wall.

'Get away from me, you horrible mongrels!' Morris yelped. 'This is SO undignified!'

Everyone listened to Morris's cries of alarm and the barking of Allegra, Electra and Olympia until it faded into silence.

'Now,' Philomena finally said, wedging her hands on her hips with a look of victory on her face. 'Who fancies a game of haunt-and-seek?'

14
SPOTTED!

The dusty days spent in the Hippodrome rolled by like the sea mists that came and went. Ella had never laughed so much in her life and she filled more notebooks than ever before with lists she never imagined writing.

She also discovered that the ghosts loved nothing more than telling and retelling the stories of how they . . . what had Madame Grebble called it . . . *kicked the chamber pot?*

The thought of dying made Ella's toes squirm, but she jotted it all down regardless.

Kicking Chamber Pots

(Note to self – DON'T READ LATE
   AT NIGHT!!)

Philomena Flummery – 'Present from
   Mr Hitler' (a BOMB in the Blitz)

Morris Gulch — Juliet's balcony collapsed on top of him (poor Morris!)

Giuseppe Stupendi — lost his legs

Madame Eudora Grebble — crusts on a cheese sandwich

Clementine Cramps — the backstage fire of 1879

Alonzo McBurnie — broken floorboard in lavatory (he fell through INTO THE SEA!)

Florrie and Vesta Tunk — the rope snapped

Tides rose and fell and the weeks slipped happily by, filled with games and stories and lots of performing. When she wasn't learning new tricks from the Tunk Twins, rehearsing scenes with Morris, or practising to sing super-high notes with Clementine Cramps, Ella liked to visit the roof with Philomena and her poodles. The two would sit for hours amongst the stone angels, talking about Aunt Sylvie, playing I-Spy and looking out over Cod's Bottom. Every moment in the theatre was another reason for Ella to fall more deeply in love with her new hometown, but she was even more excited than usual on one rainy Thursday morning.

She raced down Cuttlebone Lane, with Wilson in tow, to meet Nula, Bertie and Violet by the pier. Ignoring the drizzly weather, she bounded onto the promenade and spotted her fabulous friends instantly.

'What did your mum say?' Nula asked as Ella and Wilson trotted over.

Ella was terrible at running and had to stop to catch her breath, leaning against the railings.

'Ugh! I bet she said no,' Nula grumbled. 'I knew she would.'

'Hang on, N-Nula,' Bertie said. 'Be p-patient.'

'I bet she did,' Nula replied. 'She said no . . . you'll see.'

'So, what's the verdict, Ella?' Violet encouraged her panting friend. 'Come on, spit it out. Sleepover or no sleepover?'

'She said,' Ella huffed, feeling her pink cheeks tingling. 'She said . . . YES!'

'Yeah!' Nula cheered. 'I knew she'd say that!'

'Ha ha,' Bertie guffawed. 'You s-sound like M-Madame Grebble, Nula.'

'I did know! Deep down I *knew* she would!' Nula scowled then smiled and grabbed Ella's hand as they all took off again, heading for the Hippodrome.

For days, the children had been secretly plotting and planning a TERRIFIC sleepover at the theatre, and

Ella's mum was the last to agree to it. Of course, Ella had needed to tell a teensy-weeny (but very necessary) lie. She'd told Mum she was taking Wilson to Violet's house for a dog-grooming sleepover. She felt dreadful, but the knowledge that everyone had fibbed – all saying they were staying at each other's homes – made it a little easier to deal with.

Ella shook the guilt away, and the thought of a whole night with her ghost friends soon made her forget about lying to Mum.

'Tonight will be AMAZING!' Violet whooped as they dashed across the fishermen's yard. 'You wait, Ella! Brilliant things happen in the theatre at night, especially when it's a full moon. There's so much you haven't seen yet!'

Ella's skin bristled at the thought of what new things she might see. Nula had been talking about the wisps that rise through the floorboards, and Ella tapped her pocket as she hurried along to check her brand-new notebook was in there. She'd filled three notebooks in the past two weeks alone.

Chattering excitedly, they made their way along the harbour wall, Wilson hot on their heels, and had just squeezed through the loose railing, when a whining voice came out of nowhere and startled them all:

'What are you doing, freaks?'

Everyone spun round and found themselves staring at the sour sneer of Veronica Ratsinger. She eyed Ella like a festering blister through the bars of the gate.

'You CAN'T go in there. RULE-BREAKERS!'

Nobody replied. Ella stared back at the grimacing girl, feeling like she'd just been caught committing a terrible crime. Veronica must have followed them along the promenade. Why hadn't she glanced behind her to check no one was watching them?!?

'That hideous old dump is closed,' the ratty child went on.

'Go away, RATSULKER!' Nula finally snapped, making Wilson bark along with her. 'It's none of your business.'

'Who asked for your opinion, weirdo?' Veronica hissed at Nula. 'I'm talking to Ella the BUG-BURGER!'

'Leave us alone,' Ella said as calmly as she could, refusing to let any worry show on her face.

'SHUT UP, ALL OF YOU! My daddy runs this town and he says no one is allowed in there,' Veronica scoffed. 'So I think it is my business.'

'Your daddy is a moron,' Violet replied. 'A big one!'

'Yeah!' Bertie agreed in the bravest voice he could muster.

Veronica looked like her head was about to rocket off her shoulders. 'You'll regret that, Violet Bunkly,' she

141

hissed. 'Daddy says your family are all layabouts and scroungers, and you're exactly the same. In fact, he says ALL your families are a waste of space.'

A fire exploded in Ella's belly as she listened to the rat-faced bully. She thought of Aunt Sylvie and about the horrible things Veronica's daddy had said and felt her hands balling into fists.

'Why would you want to go into such a fleapit anyway?' Veronica jeered. 'I suppose all that dirt and mess makes you feel right at ho—'

'STOP IT, VERONICA!' Ella roared so loudly she almost frightened herself, and poor Wilson jumped so much he nearly left the floor. The little dog started barking wildly at their unwanted visitor. 'It doesn't matter what you or your daddy think, because WE DON'T CARE! We might not have a house up on the cliffs. We might not have ponies. We might not go to the best school in Cod's Bottom. But we've got something you'll never have.'

'WHAT?' Veronica yelped. 'I'll get my daddy to buy me whatever it is and mine will be bigger and better than yours, you BUG-BURGER!'

'Happiness,' Ella replied. She was trembling all over with . . . with . . . what was this brave feeling? 'We have HAPPINESS . . . and your daddy can't buy you that.'

Veronica froze, her mouth hanging open like one of

the crated sardines in the fishermen's yard.

'Now go away and bother someone else,' Ella went on (she felt rotten about telling Veronica off, but the sneering weasel deserved it), 'We're going to play in the Hippodrome, and you can't stop us by being rude about our families. Why don't you go and stand by your daddy's car park sign?' And, with that, they all turned on their heels and disappeared into the thicket of bushes that blocked the path ahead, leaving Veronica standing gobsmacked and alone at the gates.

'That was *fantastic!*' Violet whispered to Ella as they scrambled between the thorny branches. 'Ratsinger looked like she was going to wet her pants!'

Ella smiled a half-smile as she hopped over a branch. She wanted to feel victorious, so why did she feel awful instead? Her stomach tied itself into a knot and she thought about running back to the gate to apologise.

If Ella *had* turned back, she might have heard Veronica hiss, 'You think I can't stop you, you freaks? Let's see about that.' She might also have seen her pull a pink mobile phone out of her satchel and dial her daddy's number. But she didn't, and the four children ventured inside the Hippodrome without the tiniest clue of the trouble that was about to come their way.

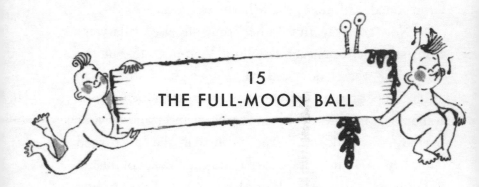

15
THE FULL-MOON BALL

'Don't turn round yet!' Violet said, waving her hand in front of Ella's eyes to make sure they were closed. 'Just two more seconds!'

Ella was standing in a shaft of moonlight at the front of the wonky Hippodrome stage with her back to all the rows of seats. Already that day they'd slid down the banisters, explored the dressing rooms at the back of the theatre, and laughed themselves silly at the sight of Wilson frantically chasing Lakshmi round the foyer, but now the sun had finally set and Ella was looking forward to seeing what magical things the night would bring out of hiding.

'What am I supposed to be doing?' she asked.

'Nothing yet,' Violet replied. 'Let me just . . .'

Ella peeked, and from the corner of her eye she saw Violet jump down from the stage and vanish into the auditorium behind her, where Bertie and Nula were waiting with the other ghosts in the aisles.

'I feel really silly. What are you up to?' Ella groaned, still facing the rear of the stage.

'You'll see, darlin',' Philomena chuckled. 'This will be a fine treat. It only happens when the theatre is sleeping under a full moon.'

'But why am I standing up here not looking at anyone?' Ella asked.

'It'll be f-fun,' said Bertie. 'I p-promise!'

'Maybe, if you like that sort of thing,' sniffed Giuseppe. 'I prefer legs.'

'Giuseppe Stupendi, stop being grumpy! You'll ruin Ella's fun,' said Alonzo. 'Ignore him, little lady.'

'I sense Alonzo thinks you're going to enjoy this one,' Madame Grebble rasped and spluttered from somewhere behind Ella. 'Lakshmi! Get away from that blasted dog! Wilson's worse than those poodles!'

'Right, are you ready?' Nula called over the other voices.

'I suppose so,' replied Ella, feeling slightly apprehensive.

'Okay. On the count of three,' Violet said, 'turn round and face us.'

'That's all?'

'That's all!'

'Here we g-go! Bertie cried. Ella could hear the

excitement in his voice. 'Ooh, I hope this works!'

'You hope what works?' Ella was starting to feel nervous.

'You'll see . . . Ready?' Nula laughed.

'Ready!'

'One, Two, THREE!' the children chorused together.

Ella braced herself and spun round to face the auditorium. Not sure what to expect, she'd thought maybe the ghosts had prepared a special new act, or Clementine would sing a song, so she nearly fell back in surprise when she turned to behold a sea of phantom faces staring at her, all glowing in the darkness like flickering candles. There were hundreds of them! Every seat in the entire theatre was filled with smartly dressed spectral men, women and children. They weren't quite as visible and brightly glowing as Ella's ghost friends, but she could see them nonetheless, packed into the crowded rows on all three levels of the theatre, and they burst into echoey applause as Ella came face to face with them.

'Surprise!' Violet yelled. 'I knew they'd appear for you, Ella!'

'WHAT!?!' Ella gazed at the hundreds of spooks as they whistled and hollered. Shimmering top hats were flung into the air and ghostly roses were thrown onto the stage around Ella's feet.

'AMAZING!' Ella shouted. *So this was what it felt like to be a famous star!*

Bertie ran to the bottom of the little steps that led from the stage to the central aisle and yelled, 'Now c-come down, Ella!'

Ella did as she was told. She put her foot onto the top step and—

'They're gone!' she gasped, shocked by how loud her voice sounded in the sudden quiet. Ella looked about and saw that every single applauding spectre had evaporated into smoke the very moment she'd taken one foot off the stage. She stepped back up onto the wonky boards and a deafening ROAR erupted again as the haunted audience sparked back into sight.

'Now they're here, now they're gone! Now they're here, now they're gone!' Ella whooped as she hopped on and off the top step, watching the crowd disappear and reappear in the blink of an eye. She stopped and looked at her friends standing in the now-empty auditorium. 'What's going on?'

'They're an audience apparition,' Nula hooted. 'Isn't it great?'

'More ghosts!' Ella beamed. 'I didn't think there was anyone left to meet.'

'Not quite ghosts,' Philomena chuckled. 'They're more like a memory that's woven into the seats.'

'Huh?' Ella wrinkled her nose in confusion.

'They can't chat to you or think like we can,' Philomena went on. 'They're like a mirage or a dream, I suppose.'

'Do you know that feeling when something triggers a recollection in your head?' Clementine asked. Ella nodded. 'Well, you standing up there on the stage just made the Hippodrome remember the good old days when there were bums in every seat.'

'The theatre's dr-dreaming!' Bertie said, grinning.

Ella tapped her toe on the wonky boards one last time and giggled as the delighted crowd flashed into view for the quickest of moments.

'Ah, how I've missed the sound of rapturous adoration,' sighed Morris, looking a little forlorn. 'The cheers, the tears, the love! Sadly, they only appear when a true living performer graces the stage on the night of a full moon – and you can imagine how often *that* happens. Hearing their joyful applause again warms my frosty cockles.'

'Violet, Bertie and Nula are living,' Ella pointed out. 'You should have asked them to stand on the stage if you missed it so much.'

'It doesn't work like that,' Violet said. 'The "true performer" part is even more important than the breathing, heart-beaty bit.'

Nula humphed. 'They've never appeared for me. They're too fussy!'

'I've only got a clap out of them once when I recited my favourite limerick,' Violet joined in. 'The one about the farmer and . . . never mind. But they only lasted for a few seconds.'

'I get a great b-big cheer when I do ro-rolly-p-pollies,' Bertie said proudly.

'Very true, darlin',' Philomena cooed, smiling at Bertie. 'They do love your acrobatics.'

'But for us ghosties and ghoulies,' said Morris, glumly, 'nothing! An audience of apparitions do not applaud the likes of us.'

'And performing to an empty house is . . .' Alonzo sniffed.

'It's miserable,' blubbed Clementine Cramps, blowing her nose on her beard.

'Rude, if you ask me,' Madame Grebble wheezed. 'We've all tried our best—'

'But our talent goes ignored,' Morris sighed, interrupting the old psychic, who glared at him over her spectacles.

'Oh, Morris.' Ella looked at the sadness in the actor-ghost's eyes and suddenly thought she might cry.

'They loved *you* though, darlin',' Philomena said. 'Just as we knew they would. Bravo!'

Ella smiled and enjoyed the electric tingle of knowing

150

that the spectral audience thought she was a true performer, and she understood the sting of pain that her ghost friends must have felt having no one to entertain.

'Show people need an audience,' Ella said, thinking for a moment, and then held her hand out towards Morris. 'Here.'

The gangly ghost adjusted his top hat and raised an eyebrow. 'I'm not sure what you want me to do,' he muttered.

'I know you can't actually hold my hand, but pretend. Just for fun.'

Morris looked at Philomena, who shrugged. 'Very well,' he said with a curious smirk. 'I'm never one to turn down a spot of make-believe acting, you know? I am the Bard of Bermondsey, after all.'

The tall ghost lowered his gravely cold hand into Ella's palm, taking care not to stick it straight through. She looked down and shivered, watching ice crystals crackle across her skin.

'What now, Miss Griffin?'

'Follow me, Morris,' said Ella, guiding him up onto the stage and depositing him at the front of the wooden boards. 'You wait here.'

Ella walked all the way to the back wall of the stage and stood there, facing towards the corner. 'Okay. I want you to deliver your most heart-wrenching speech. Something really big and dramatic,' she called over her shoulder.

'But you're not watching,' Morris grunted.

'I'm listening,' Ella said. 'Perform for Violet, Bertie and Nula. Do a tragic one . . . or something adventurous. Wilsy loves Shakespeare.'

'Very well.' The ghost paused for a moment, taking a few deep breaths. 'I shall recite a little *Macbeth*.'

'You can't say that word inside a theatre!' Clementine Cramps gasped, fanning herself with her wispy hand. 'It's bad luck!'

'We're already dead, you fool!' Morris shot back at her. 'Things can't get much worse, can they?'

'Concentrate!' Ella ordered, trying not to giggle. 'Now, go for it, Octavius P. Gulch – show us what you're made of!'

Morris began his speech and Ella listened. She didn't know *Macbeth* very well – Mum insisted it was a bit too scary and grown-up to read yet – but it sounded exciting! There was talk of witches, and a floating dagger, and spots that wouldn't vanish . . . whatever that meant.

Morris cursed and plotted, and wailed and cried, and acted his unbeating heart out in his best Shakespearian voice. He was just coming to a booming climax, his arms outstretched to the heavens when . . .

HOORAY! WOO-HOO! MORE! ENCORE!

152

Making sure she was out of Morris's eyeline, Ella had turned to face the auditorium, and the audience had instantly appeared, cheering and clapping wildly.

Ella fought back a sob as she saw the ghost jolt with joyful, startled surprise. He gazed out at the clamouring onlookers as they threw flowers and gave a standing ovation, before taking a small bow.

'Thank you! Thank you!' Morris cried as he scooped up armfuls of see-through roses. He turned to Ella in the far corner of the stage. 'And thank *YOU*, Miss Griffin.' There were tears of ectoplasm glistening on his cheeks and his green eyes softened with a glow of total happiness.

Ella grinned at the ghost. It felt lovely, giving him a moment to shine. She glanced at her new friends standing in the aisles of the theatre with hundreds of cheering phantoms bustling around them.

'My go next!' Clementine shrieked, grabbing the petticoats of her ballgown and hurrying through the air to the stage.

'I want a turn too!' Alonzo whooped.

'I bet they'd love my legs!' wept Giuseppe. 'My heart would break . . . if I had one.'

'Us! Please!' The Tunk Twins shouted even louder.

'Oh, stop all your clamourin'!' Philomena shouted over the chaotic gaggle of ghosts. 'Park your peepers on that!' She pointed to the hole in the ceiling and everybody looked up.

'Wow!' Ella ran to the front of the stage. The spectral audience roared in her ears, but this time she took no notice of them. Moonlight was now streaming in, as the full moon positioned itself right above the Hippodrome, illuminating everything in the auditorium with delicate, shimmering outlines.

'It's time,' Philomena said, trembling with excitement. In the silvery light, she glowed brighter than Ella had ever seen before, and she looked wonderful. 'The full moon is above us and the crowds have arrived. LET

154

THE FULL-MOON BALL BEGIN!'

Ella watched the night slide gracefully by in a twinkling, dreamlike haze. After she took one final bow for the audience apparition, all the spectral men and women had risen from their seats and began waltzing down the aisles and through the air as the orchestra played.

'I told you it was good,' Violet said as she sat down next to Ella and Wilson at the front of the stage, offering them a sandwich from her lunchbox.

'I never ever dreamed I'd see anything like this,' Ella replied.

'It's not over yet,' Violet said, patting the stage boards they were sitting on. 'Look!'

Ella glanced down and noticed the cracks between the wooden planks were glowing. 'What is it?' she asked. 'What's that light?'

'This is my favourite part.' Violet beamed. She wriggled her finger over one of the wonky gaps in the stage and Ella gasped as lots of tiny lights began floating up around her hand, dancing in the air like tropical fish around coral. They had the appearance of little blue candle flames, but without the candles.

'What are they?' Ella asked, her eyes wide.

'Wisps!' Violet laughed. 'They're the fireflies of the ghost world.' She stood up and twirled on the spot as hundreds of the flickering lights burst up through the

155

cracks and swirled around her like a glowing whirlpool.

'This is brilliant!' Ella scrambled to her feet, giggling and chattering as shimmering wisps surrounded her and Wilson, making the squat dog bark wildly. 'Look, Wilsy – isn't it amazing!' She looked around happily at the waltzing spectres spinning overhead, and the twinkling lights, and the full moon above, and her friends laughing, and at Wilson bounding off the stage to chase Lakshmi, and the ballerina twirling into view in the central aisle, and—

'GISELLE! WAIT!' Ella jumped down the steps,

leaping straight through a ghostly couple as they glided past. She sprinted along the aisle towards the elusive ballerina. 'Please, wait!'

The ghostly girl, who was in the middle of a spectacular leap, stopped in mid-air and stared at Ella.

'Giselle! I need to talk to you! You knew my aunt – is that why you came to see me? Why you were in my room?'

It was no use. Before Ella could reach her, the ballerina turned and flew swiftly towards the rear of the auditorium.

'Don't go!' Ella cried over the loud orchestra music. As more and more apparitions danced past, she gave up ducking and simply ran through them, tingling with frost. 'Please – wait for me!'

Just before Giselle flew through the back wall of the theatre, she stopped by a row of framed posters, like the ones Ella had seen in the hallway, and . . . did Ella imagine it, or did the ghostly dancer turn back to look at her, then point to one of the frames on the far left of the row?

There was a fleeting moment when everything seemed to slow down as Giselle's eyes met Ella's, and then she was gone, straight through the poster she'd pointed to.

'Oh, bum!' Violet huffed as she caught up with Ella at the end of the aisle. 'I don't know why Giselle's so shy. She's never spoken to me either – and I mean NEVER.'

'I think . . .' Ella wrinkled her forehead in concentration, trying to block out the noise of the ball. 'I think she wanted to tell me something.'

'I doubt it,' Violet said. 'She doesn't really want to say anything at all, I don't thi—'

Ella walked away from her friend towards the framed poster that Giselle had just flown through. The glass was frosted and tiny icicles dangled from the bottom of it.

'This one!' Ella turned and called to Violet. 'She pointed to this.'

By now, Nula and Bertie had spotted that something was happening at the back of the vast room and had run along a row of seats to join Ella and Violet at the frozen picture.

'W-what's going on?' Bertie asked.

'Ella saw the ballerina,' Violet said. 'But she got away.'

'So?' Nula shrugged. 'We're missing the party!'

'Giselle pointed to this poster and then disappeared through it,' Ella said. She pulled the cuff of her jumper over her hand and wiped away the ice that crackled across it, exposing an advert for a variety act that Ella hadn't spotted before.

'"The Jenkins Sisters",' she read aloud, practically screaming. '"Giselle and Evelyn Jenkins. Swanlike ballerinas"!'

'Why is that so exciting?' Nula asked.

'Miss Jenkins!' Ella yelped, instantly recognising her wrinkly neighbour as one of the young faces on the poster. She'd changed so much, but there was no mistaking those eyes. 'Miss Jenkins is Giselle's sister! She's still alive and lives in the flat above ours!'

16
THE SEARCH BEGINS

'Did you try the cloakrooms, darlin'?' Philomena asked as she floated up the staircase ahead of Ella and Wilson. 'Not that I've ever seen her haunting around there, but it's worth a peek.'

Allegra and Electra were busy yapping all over the place in pursuit of the mysterious ballerina. They kept disappearing and reappearing through walls, while Olympia flew up to sit on the broken chandelier and lazily licked the curly fur on her paw, clearly not in the mood for a spot of hunt-the-spook.

'I looked there twice!' Ella groaned as she squinted against the daylight that now streamed in through the grimy atrium windows. 'It's practically morning and we've looked everywhere.'

'D'you know, Giselle became a ghost the same night I did, the poor lamb,' Philomena sighed. 'Not going into any gory details, but we were both performing that night Mr Hitler dropped one of his boom-bangers straight through the roof. And to think her sister still lives in Cod's Bottom! I can remember 'em together, always giggling and whispering. Giselle never said anything about it to us.'

'She doesn't say anything at all,' one of the orchestra ghosts piped up as he rushed past.

'I think I'm starting to understand,' Ella replied, glancing over the banister and watching other ghosts zipping about on the lower levels of the theatre.

Alonzo MacBurnie was standing in the centre of the foyer, yelling Giselle's name, and Clementine Cramps had enlisted the help of a gaggle of last night's wisps from the basement. The little blue flames flickered around her like moths, lighting her way as she joined in the search on the first floor.

'We've looked in the ticket office and the ground floor loos,' Clementine informed them. 'Where can she be?'

'Don't you panic, dearies. My girls will sniff her out.' Philomena stopped on the second-floor landing and looked around. 'Now, if I was a shy ballerina who doesn't talk to nobody, where would I be haunting?'

'I'm afraid she's not in the dressing rooms, Miss Griffin,' Morris called as he climbed the stairs behind her. 'I even checked beneath the stage, but the only thing I saw down there was Mr Stupendi's legs!'

'My legs!' Giuseppe's voice sobbed from some unseen place. 'Come to papa, *per favore!*'

'This is hopeless,' Nula groaned. She'd been inside the auditorium on the grand balcony, but now pushed her way back through the double doors and grimaced in Ella's direction. 'Maybe Giselle just doesn't care?'

'I'm sure she cares,' Ella replied. 'Giselle wanted me to see that poster. Maybe it's why she was in my room – maybe she was trying to get a message to Miss Jenkins.'

'She isn't anywhere!' Violet huffed as she and Bertie marched out of the grand bar.

'I suppose Giselle do-doesn't want to be f-found.'

'Oh, come now, kiddies,' Philomena said, giving Ella a reassuring wink. 'Giselle won't have gone far. She'll be moping about somewhere. We've just got to keep looking for the poor lass.'

Ella opened her mouth to speak but was interrupted by an unexpected explosion of ectoplasm right in front of her. She jumped back and had to grab hold of the banister to stop herself from tumbling down the stairs.

'I've got it!' Madame Grebble was suddenly in the middle of the small crowd, gesturing wildly and jangling her bracelets.

'What have you got, madam?' Morris scoffed as he floated up the stairs to join them. 'Wind? Or just bad breath? Both, probably.'

'Madame Grebble knows how to find the leaping lady,' the ancient ghost rasped. 'Lakshmi coughed up a phantom furball just now and I saw the answer in its many knots and lumps . . .'

'Disgusting,' Morris said flatly, 'but do go on.'

'My old mate Delilah will know where she's got to.'

Morris snorted. 'Who's Delilah?'

'Delilah!' Madame Grebble jangled her bracelets again for dramatic effect.

'There's no such person!'

'Yes, there is!'

'She's making things up for the attention,' said Morris, rolling his eyes. 'Just ignore her.'

'Oh, go and stick your head inside a rock!' Madame Grebble yelled with such gusto, she spat out her ghostly dentures again.

'We don't know a Delilah, darlin',' Philomena said, patting Grebble on the shoulder. 'Are you sure you're not just a little bit confused?'

'Get off!' the fortune teller snapped. 'You younglings haven't got a clue. Delilah! The Damsel of the Dark! Maiden of the Middle! She's been watching you nincompoops collie-shangling about for over a hundred years and knows everything that comes and goes in this place. We have a gossip every second Monday of the month.'

Ella watched as each ghost shook their head. They clearly had no idea what the gristly old ghost was waffling on about.

'Too wrapped up in your own stupid business, you self-centred bunch of blatherskites!' Madame Grebble barked. 'Anyway –' she turned to Ella and peered over the top of her glasses – 'don't you worry. Delilah will know where she's hiding.'

Ella watched, feeling more confused by the second, as Madame Grebble swivelled round to face the centre of the grand atrium and shouted over the gallery balustrade: 'Pendle, my lump, are you there?' There was a moment of silence until a strange squeaking noise caught everyone's attention. It was the sound of someone writing on glass with their finger. Ella turned just in time to see the word **YES** being spelled out in the dust on a nearby mirror. This was followed by **TEA, ANYONE?**

'Oh, there you are, Pendle!' Madame Grebble chuckled. 'No tea now, dearie – I need a favour. The kiddywinkles have to visit Delilah. Couldn't give us a hand or two, could you?'

As if in answer to Madame Grebble's request, Ella and her three friends were instantly lifted off their feet in a great rush of dust and pigeon feathers, as if a sea squall wind was blowing straight up through the floor.

'Agh! What's going on?' Ella yelped. She wasn't ready to find herself plucked into the air, and accidentally kicked a leg through Philomena's stomach and out the other side. 'Oops. Sorry, Philly!'

'No harm done,' Philomena replied, looking utterly fascinated with what was happening. 'Well I never! You're floating just like a ghost, Ella.'

'Can you put us down, please, Pendle?' It was the strangest

feeling Ella had ever experienced. As the poltergeist held her in place, her toes dangling just above the mouldy carpet, Ella could feel invisible hands under her arms and supporting her back. How many hands did Pendle have?

'Where are we going?' gasped Violet as she hovered right next to Ella.

'I'm n-not sure about this,' Bertie whimpered. He reached out and grabbed Violet's elbow as Pendle nudged him between the two girls.

'Woo-hoo!' Nula threw her arms above her head like she was on a roller coaster, laughing excitedly when she bumped against Ella's hip. 'This is going to be good! I feel like a superhero! Can we do a loop-the-loop, Pendle?'

'Marvellous stuff.' Madame Grebble cackled at the levitating children and rubbed her gnarled hands together like a villain in one of Ella's comic books. 'Righty-ho, off we go!'

There was barely enough time to let out a startled scream before Ella and her friends sped across the second-floor gallery, gliding straight through Morris with a sparkle of ectoplasm and a tingle of frost, heading for the double doors that led to the auditorium.

'Poltergeists are so useful,' Grebble tittered as she flew alongside the children. 'Always keep one handy, that's what I say. This way, lovies.'

Ella watched as the old ghost vanished through the wall next to the auditorium doors and she braced herself for the inevitable painful bump of smashing into the heavy wooden things.

'We're not dead, Pendle!' Violet yelped. 'We can't fly throu—'

Just as it looked like they were going to crash, the double doors swung open and the children sped into the darkness of the now spectre-less grand balcony, leaving Wilson barking frantically behind them.

'You took your time,' Madame Grebble croaked from among the rows of empty seats when Ella and her friends finally flew into view. 'Come on, dearies, follow me.'

'Stop! Stop! STOP!' Bertie squealed as Pendle carried them out across the seats and into the wide-open space beyond the edge of the balcony railing. 'Please d-don't drop us!'

'What are you doing?' Ella cried, her heart thundering in her chest She chanced a quick look downwards and instantly regretted it, thinking for one dreadful moment she might be sick. They were floating high above the central aisle of the auditorium, drifting through the dust-filled beam of light from the broken roof and heading towards the proscenium arch. 'I don't like heights!' Ella screamed. 'WE'RE GOING TO DIE!'

'I sense you're a bit worried,' Grebble wheezed as she tried to keep up with Pendle and the four flying children. 'Don't panic – we're almost there.'

'Almost where?' blubbed Violet. She was frozen with terror and had her eyes clamped firmly shut.

'Here!' Grebble chuckled contentedly.

'Cor!' Nula cooed. She didn't seem to mind the enormous drop below them at all. 'Look at this, guys!'

Ella glanced up from the terrifying view and saw they had come to a stop right in front of the great carved archway over the stage. She'd never seen the frolicking cherubs and lounging angels this close up before and almost immediately forgot her fear as she took in all the incredible detail.

'Lovely, ain't it?' Madame Grebble said with a toothless grin. She pointed to a tiny cherub with puffed-out cheeks blowing on a curved horn. 'He's my favourite. *Pffft!*'

'What are we doing up here?' Violet squeaked. 'I want to go back!'

'Calm down, dear!' Grebble replied. 'Now, girls and . . . err . . . boy, I'd like you to meet my old friend Delilah.' She gestured to the very centre of the proscenium arch, where both sides met in the middle, forming the ornately carved shape of a beautiful woman's head and shoulders.

The four children stared at the woman's pale cracked face and waited.

Nothing . . .

'Delilah, darlin', we've come to see you.'

Nothing . . .

'Is something supposed to happen?' Nula asked.

'Delilah, wake up!' Grebble grumbled. 'Now's not the time to be snoozin'.'

The children waited again and still nothing happened.

'Oi! You're embarrassing me.'

'Madame Grebble,' Ella mumbled. 'You know that's not a real person, don't you? She's made of plaster. She can't talk.'

'Can't talk? Don't be so foolish, dearie, of course she can talk. Are you fuddled?' Madame Grebble humphed. 'Boy, do me a weensy favour and give her a tickle, will you?'

'W-what?' Bertie stammered. 'I can't!'

'Course, you can. Grab a feather or something,' Grebble went on. 'There's a bunch of 'em tangled in the spiderwebs. That'll wake up the lazybones.'

169

Bertie looked at his friends for reassurance, got none, then reached out a visibly shaking hand to pluck a tatty pigeon feather from the cobwebs dangling off a nearby cherub's harp.

'That's right,' Madame Grebble encouraged him. 'Now, tickle her nose with it. She won't like that one bit. Ha ha!'

'Um, o-k-kay . . .' Bertie leaned towards the lifeless woman's face, panicked as he wobbled over the enormous drop, and shoved the entire feather up Delilah's left nostril.

'BLEUGH!' The carved head suddenly recoiled with a loud cracking noise, shaking this way and that and wafting a thick cloud of dust around her. She opened her mouth wide, coughing and wheezing as a flurry of moths flew out. 'Argh! Get off! What have you done to me?'

'There you are!' Madame Grebble clapped happily. 'Didn't I tell you, kiddies?'

Ella couldn't have replied if she'd wanted to. As the cloud around Delilah started to clear, she saw for the first time that the plaster woman was actually gold underneath all the dirt! Her pale, ghostly skin had just been the thick layer of dust that had settled all over her.

'Oh no! Oh n-n-no!' Bertie yelped as the head spluttered in his face. He didn't know what to do and started scrabbling in mid-air, trying to get away from

170

the snorting statue that now had a feather hanging out of her hooter.

The head snuffled – 'Take it out! It tickles! IT TICKLES!'

'AGH!' Bertie screamed.

'Get out of the way, Bertster!' Nula gently pushed him aside, then leaned across Violet and Ella. 'Hold on, won't be a sec.' She grabbed the stalk of the feather and yanked it out of Delilah's nostril. 'There!' she said. 'Is that better?'

'Who d'you blooming well think you are?' the golden lady snapped at Bertie. 'Waking me up from a delicious dream, stuffing flotsam up my conk!'

'S-sorry!' Bertie grimaced. 'Madame Grebble told me to do it. I d-didn't m-mean any harm.'

'Madame Grebble? Is that grizzled harpy here?' The head swivelled round and glared at the ancient ghost. 'Ah, there you are, Eudora. Is it the second Monday of the month already? What's the goss?'

'Not this time, my crumbly chum,' Madame Grebble said warmly. 'Now you've finished ignoring us, we need a few questions answering, Delilah.'

'I wasn't ignoring you,' Delilah corrected. 'You know our rules, Grebble. Us carvings aren't supposed to let humans see us on the move. It only causes trouble.'

'These four are different,' said Madame Grebble,

nodding to Ella and her friends. 'This lot are honorary ghosties of the theatre. They're allowed to see.'

Delilah turned her smooth golden eyes on the floating children and stared. Then she raised a flaking eyebrow. 'Well, well, well,' she said. A tiny smile crept into the corner of her cracked mouth. 'Very interesting indeed.'

17
RUMBLINGS

'Oh, it must have been nearly eighty years since I last chatty-wagged to one of you humans!' Delilah tittered. 'Yonks and yonkers! It was a man on a scaffold trying to clean the chandeliers, if my musty memory is correct. The poor gawper nearly fell off his perch and joined the spooks when I bid him good morning.'

The children stared at the talking head in the gloom and didn't say a word in return. Ella gave her forehead a tiny tap with her fingertip, trying to figure out if she was dreaming. This was even weirder than the total weirdness of having ghosts for friends. At least ghosts made sense. They were the souls of people who had lived long ago and had popped their clogs, but what was this gossiping statue all about?

'I hope you don't mind me asking,' Ella said, trying her hardest not to upset the carved woman, 'but how are you talking, Delilah? You're made from plaster and gold paint.'

'Wrong!' Delilah replied. 'I'm made from theatre.'

'I . . . I don't understand.'

'I'm part of this place – the Hippodrome. We all are, aren't we, fellas?'

Ella let out a yelp as every cherub and angel on the proscenium arch swivelled its head in Ella's direction and nodded in agreement, causing more clouds of choking dust to lift and swirl about, and revealing the gold paintwork that lay beneath it.

'That's right, Delilah!'

'Yep!'

'You're spot on there.'

Ella nearly burst out laughing. 'I knew it!' she blurted.

'Knew what?' Delilah asked.

'I knew the cherubs above the entrance turned to look at me on the first day I came here. They were watching the gate one minute and then staring at me tripping through the bushes the next. I thought I must have imagined it!'

Delilah grunted and her mouth curved downwards into a scowl. 'They'll be getting a serious talking-to in that case!' she snapped. 'I'm the chief cherub around here and that's definitely against the rules, make no mistake!'

'Oh.' Ella pulled a worried face. She hadn't meant to get any cherubs into trouble. She also didn't want to stay high up in the air a moment longer than they needed to. 'Er, anyway . . . you were saying?'

'Hmmm,' Delilah added grumpily. 'Well, as I was explaining before I was so rudely interrupted: we theatre folk are made of this place, and this place is made of us. That's why I can talk just like the griping ghosts who haunt the Hippodrome's rooms. It's the same for all of us, you see.'

But Ella didn't see, not really . . .

'All buildings have memories,' Delilah went on. 'This theatre's got more than most, and those memories are in our heads. The walls remember everything that's happened here, and we're part of the walls. Cobwebs whisper, and we're covered in the blinkin' things. Every rattling window, creaking floorboard, dripping tap or groaning staircase is the theatre having a gossip, and we're just another gossiping part of it. The only difference is that we cherubs natter in a language you can understand. Got it?'

Ella nodded, even though she wasn't sure she understood at all.

'So now we've cleared that up, what can old Delilah help you children with today?' the carved woman cooed with an impish smile.

'We're looking for someone,' Nula said. 'It's important we find them.'

'Ugh! Why are you bothering me then?' Delilah grumbled, her face dropping into a frown again. 'I just told you I haven't seen human-types in nearly eighty years.'

'No, we're not looking for a human,' said Violet, still trembling and trying desperately not to look down. 'We're searching for a ghost.'

'And sh-she's somewhere in the th-theatre,' Bertie added.

'Ohhhh! Why didn't you say so?' Delilah's mood seemed to instantly brighten. If she hadn't been missing a body entirely, Ella could have sworn she saw the gold woman sit up with interest. 'Who? Who? Who are you looking for? It's been ages since I've had something to do.'

'Her name is Giselle,' Ella said. 'She haunts this place, but keeps herself hidden away. I saw her on my first visit to the theatre, but we can't find her now, and we really need to talk to her. It's important.'

'Hmm, interesting . . .' Delilah said, creasing up her forehead with a crumbly cracking sound. 'Let me have a little search about.' She closed her eyes and started humming. 'This one could be a real challenge.'

The children watched as Delilah's head bobbed

from side to side while she muttered to herself, like she was sifting through old thoughts, trying to recall a dusty memory.

'Giselle . . . Giselle . . . Giselle . . . where are you?'

'What's she doing?' Nula whispered to Madame Grebble as the mumbling went on.

'Delilah's not just a head and neck – the whole theatre is her body, y'see?' the fortune teller replied. 'She feels all the goings-on around here, like you'd feel an ant crawling on your arm. Very clever stuff.'

'Very ticklish stuff, when those pesky spook-pooches are snuffling around backstage,' Delilah added, sneakily opening one eye.

'Spook-pooches,' Bertie giggled. 'SPOOCHES!'

'No sign of her in the old stage manager's office,' Delilah said, her eyes firmly closed again. 'There's a slight tickle in one of the dressing rooms, but that's only a family of rats who've made a home in the laundry hamper.'

'We already looked there anyway,' Violet said blankly.

'Now you tell me,' Delilah scoffed. She continued bobbing her head from side to side, wiggling her eyebrows and muttering under her breath. 'Nothing but musical manifestations in the orchestra pit. There's only whiffy-waifs and a few unsavoury souls flickering about in the lavatory. Oh . . . I can feel there's a crowd

177

of ghosts and lots of fussing about in the second-floor gallery, and – wait . . . is that a LIVING DOG with them? Could your Giselle be there?'

'No, that's where the others are waiting,' said Nula. 'It's Philomena and Morris—'

'And Alonzo, Giuseppe and Clementine,' said Violet.

'And W-W-Wilson,' added Bertie.

Delilah kept her eyes shut. 'Seems like they're all bickering. The tall gentleman is having a right good moan, and the bearded woman is pacing about. Now – ugh! Hold on a second . . .'

Ella watched as Delilah's beautiful face started to twitch.

'Is that . . . I think . . . HA! GOT HER!' she whooped. 'There's a slight tingly itch coming from . . .'

'From where?' Ella blurted. 'Where is she?'

'Oh, it's ever so faint. She's barely there at all. You were very lucky to see this ghost even the once, young lady.' Delilah opened her eyes and stared at Ella. 'The spook ballerina you're looking for is on the roof, staring at the town, all sad, like. She's there right now. The Maiden of the Middle – that's me – is never wro—'

'What are we waiting for?' Ella interrupted. 'I mean . . . thank you so much, Delilah. You've been incredibly helpful, but we should get moving straight away.'

'Ella's right,' Bertie said. 'This has been fun, D-Delilah.

Really scary, but f-fun. We should d-definitely be going n-now though.'

'Be off with you then!' Delilah looked disappointed and humphed loudly. 'Leave me alone in the dark again, why don't you! I'll just natter to the spiders and dead flies instead, and that'll be *way* more interesting, I'm sure.'

'Stop your nonsense, Delilah,' Madame Grebble chuckled. 'Don't forget I'll be back next week for our regular spot of gossip.'

'I'm not talking about you, Eudora,' replied Delilah sulkily. 'It's been ages since I last gossiped to a human, and you younglings want to hurry away in search of some moany, mopey, prancy ballerin— AGH!'

The golden woman's face had suddenly contorted as a look of shock and confusion spread across it.

'NO! Not that!' she exclaimed.

'What's the matter?' Madame Grebble squawked, looking very flustered. 'Stop it, you'll worry the kidlings.'

'It can't be!' Delilah gasped. Her golden eyes darted this way and that and she craned her neck like she was trying to listen to something far away.

'Are you all right?' asked Nula.

'There's a crowd of people outside,' Delilah shrieked. Her eyes were now so wide cracks had formed at their edges. 'Living people!'

'An audience!' Madame Grebble cheered.

'No, an army dressed in yellow. I can hear the pigeons on the roof cooing about it. They're frightened!'

'What rot!' Madame Grebble chuckled. She tried to smile, but her face quickly drooped into a concerned frown. 'Don't be such a foozler. There are no armies! Cod's Bottomers never come to this old place.'

'Men and women in strange yellow vests are marching towards us as we speak,' Delilah shrieked. 'We're under attack!'

The cherubs and angels along the top of the arch started crying out in alarm—

'They've broken through the gates!'

'They're at the doors!'

'The ground is shaking!'

A distant crash suddenly rumbled through the theatre and echoed round the auditorium. The sound made Ella's heart leap into her throat and her teeth began chattering. 'What was that?' she blurted to her friends. Nula and Violet shook their heads and Bertie grabbed Ella's hand in fear.

'They're here!' Delilah wailed as more cracks snaked across her horror-stricken face. 'This is the end of us. THE END!'

Madame Grebble peered at Ella over the top of her spectacles, her face betraying her mounting panic.

'I didn't sense this, girl,' she croaked. 'QUICK!'

18
MY DADDY IS A COUNCILLOR!

As Pendle carried the children back to the second-floor gallery, they were met by Philomena, who had her finger pressed to her lips. Allegra, Electra and Olympia were huddled together behind her legs, and Wilson had joined them. They were all whimpering.

'Don't make a sound,' Philomena mouthed, then pointed to the balustrade and beckoned Ella and her friends to follow her.

Pendle lowered them gently onto the threadbare carpet and Ella felt the invisible hands under her arms dissolve into nothing and vanish. She tiptoed towards the railing, found a gap between Morris and Clementine Cramps, and peered down into the atrium below.

'Look at this mess!' a gruff male voice barked.

'I'm surprised it hasn't fallen down already,' a female voice joked in reply.

Two workers in bright yellow vests were standing in the middle of the marble floor, right beneath the grimy chandelier.

'An army in yellow,' Ella murmured to herself. 'Delilah was right.' There may have only been two workers standing in the foyer, but she could hear many other voices yelling to each other, banging tools and operating machinery outside the theatre. *There must be loads of them!*

'I've seen nicer rubbish heaps,' the woman continued. She lifted her hard hat, scratched her head and chuckled. 'Everything's rotten!'

'It'll make things easier,' the man said. He was holding something round and metallic in his hand, and he absent-mindedly tossed it into the air and caught it again. Ella recognised the object immediately as one of the brass handles from the red-and-gold entrance doors.

'These people work for the council,' Nula whispered, through Clementine's enormous mass of petticoats. 'They fixed the cobbles outside my mum's shop.'

'Maybe they're going to fix the theatre?' Morris guessed hopefully. 'It could certainly use a little spruce-up here and there.'

Ella didn't reply. She couldn't explain it, but just seeing the broken door handle in the man's dirt-stained hands made her want to howl like a wild beast and defend the Hippodrome. She was furious!

'This place'll fall down like a stack of cards on a windy day,' the man said, wandering over to one of the pillars and giving it a push. 'No problem.'

Ella jolted. What was he talking about? The theatre – falling down?

A shaft of daylight suddenly extended along the length of the atrium floor, illuminating the two workers in its glare like rabbits caught in a car's headlamps.

'Is that you, boss?' The woman turned and peered into the light, shielding her eyes with one hand like she was saluting. 'You weren't kidding about this dump!'

'Indeed,' came the muttered reply from the ticket office vestibule. The voice was eerily familiar, and Ella had a sneaking suspicion she knew exactly who it belonged to.

It was just then, as his footsteps grew louder, that the third figure strode into view and headed to the very centre of the atrium. The boss had arrived. Ratzilla himself!

'I want the demolition to start immediately!' he declared. 'We cannot wait a moment longer.'

Ella's heart thundered in her chest. *Demolition!* The word rattled through her skeleton and set her teeth on edge.

'Knock it all down!' Councillor Ratsinger sneered. He flipped a sheet of paper over on his clipboard and eyed the plans that were printed upon it. 'Our town will be rid of this repulsive eyesore. My multistorey car park will be far more useful than a silly theatre.' The weasel-like man nodded to himself and straightened his grey tie. He said the word *theatre* like it left a sour tang.

'You're the boss, boss,' said the man holding the broken doorknob.

'We can get the cranes up and ready in a jiffy,' the woman joined in. 'This place'll be as flat as a pancake in no time at all. Wrecking ball swings at noon tomorrow.'

'Perfect!'

Ella could barely breathe. She stared at the three intruders and felt her anger burning furiously like nothing she'd ever experienced before. A bonfire raged in her belly and she wanted to spit red-hot coals at them for daring to *think* they could demolish the Hippodrome! It wasn't even theirs to knock down – it belonged to Philly and Morris and Delilah and to all the ghosts and cherubs, and to Violet, Bertie and Nula and, well, to her! It belonged to anyone who loved it, and no joyless bore was going to take it from them!

'A little warning would have been appreciated, dear, if you don't mind!'

Ella jumped in surprise and, seeing Clementine fanning herself with an embarrassed look on her face, she realised she'd walked straight through her and was heading for the staircase in a daze. What was she doing?

She couldn't chase the ratty man and his workers out of the theatre, could she?

'Where are you going?' whispered Violet.

'They can't do this,' Ella mouthed back. 'They can't hurt the Hippodrome.' Nervousness gushed through her veins as she clutched the banister and readied herself to dash downstairs and confront the man with his stupid clipboard. What kind of MONSTER would want to replace a theatre with a car park?!

'DADDY!'

The shrill voice was enough to stop Ella in her tracks and make her abandon her idea of confronting Ratman in an instant.

'There you are, Daddy!'

Ella stepped back towards the railing and looked down into the foyer again. Ratsinger dismissed the two demolition workers, then turned to face his daughter as her shadow appeared across the floor. 'Ah, Veronica, you're here,' he said cheerlessly.

'Will you knock it down straight away, Daddy?' Now Veronica, dressed in a frilly party frock and matching pink hard hat, ran into view. 'I want to watch it fall into the sea! Can I?'

A disgusting taste rose into Ella's mouth, along with the memory of meeting Veronica for the first time outside the post office.

'*My daddy is a councillor. He's going to transform this stupid little town.*' How was Ratzilla going to transform the town by building a CAR PARK!?

'I hate theatres,' Ratsinger said to his daughter. 'Great big wastes of space, filled with nonsense and tomfoolery.'

'Who does he think he is?' Morris quietly gasped, but Philomena silenced him, slapping a haunted hand over his mouth.

'When is it going to be knocked down, Daddy?' Veronica whined again. 'I want to see it crumple! That'll teach Ella Griffin and her freaky friends to take on a Ratsinger!' The girl seemed to be buzzing with glee.

'Indeed.' Ratzilla nodded. 'And I'll soon be a Member of Parliament – just think of the other councillors' faces . . .' He closed his eyes, breathed in deeply and sneered. 'Me, Norman Ratsinger, representing Cod's Bottom and the district of Upper Haddock Norton in the House of Commons – marvellous!'

'You'll be so powerful, Daddy, and then I'll grow up to be prime

minister and . . . and I can tell everyone what to do. I'll probably be rich too . . . richer!' Veronica cackled. 'Everyone in town is going to be super impressed when they know my daddy is knocking down this stupid old stink hole.'

It was just at that moment, as she stared on in disbelief, that Ella shivered violently. She blinked as if waking up from a bad dream, glanced over her shoulder, and realised the second-floor gallery had practically turned into the North Pole.

'Rottlers!' Madame Grebble was wheezing, as ice crystals danced about her in the dusty air. 'Ratbags and pigeon-livered hornswoggles, the lot of 'em!'

'Heartless wretches!' Morris growled.

'What's a car park?' asked Alonzo.

Ella watched her ghost friends glowering at the Ratsingers below. As they fumed, sheets of frost spread along the tatty carpets and up the walls, and everything suddenly prickled with icicles. They hung from the light fittings and stuck out from the balustrade at jagged angles like teeth.

'It's over,' Vesta Tunk sighed as tears of ectoplasm ran down her cheeks.

'The end of us,' Florrie wept.

'I think I—' but Clementine fainted before she'd finished her sentence and vanished straight through the floorboards to the gallery below.

Shrill laughter sliced through the moment of distress and sadness happening two floors above as Veronica hugged her father round his waist.

'It's horrible in here – let's go,' the councillor muttered. He shuddered in the sudden cold. 'The sooner this place is torn down, the better.'

With that, the intruders turned on their polished heels and walked towards the broken doors, dragging behind them the last scraps of happiness that belonged to a gaggle of flabbergasted ghosts and four extremely stunned friends.

19
OH, POOK!

After the Ratsingers had sloped off to enjoy their day, the ghosts and children hid themselves away from the demolition workers who were now crawling all over the Hippodrome. To avoid being seen, they had bundled themselves into the shadows of an old storeroom, where they could peer down through a dirty window to watch the workmen in the theatre's grounds below.

'This is the worst day of my afterlife!' Clementine Cramps plucked a ghostly handkerchief from the air and blew her nose loudly. 'I was planning on practising my wailing on the stairs this afternoon. Now what am I going to do?'

'They're about to knock down the Hippodrome . . . and that's all you can think about?' Morris cried. 'I'm surrounded by simpletons!' He tried to sit down on the edge of a hamper filled with mildew-stained costumes and tutted angrily when his bottom slipped straight through it.

'W-What are we g-going to do?' asked Bertie.

'They can't just destroy the theatre,' Nula said. 'Can they?'

'Oh, pook! This is bad,' Madame Grebble grunted as Lakshmi appeared in an explosion of ectoplasm. The glowing cat sauntered across the room and leaped up onto the fortune teller's shoulder, mewing nervously. 'What's to be done, Lakshmi, dear?'

'Don't bother asking the cat! You tell us!' Morris turned his rage on Madame Grebble. 'You're the psychic!'

'I'm going to boot you in the back-bits, you—'

'All right! That's enough hollerin', the pair of you!' Philomena raised her hands and stopped the arguing ghosts, mid-sentence. 'It's bad enough the Hippodrome is being destroyed without you two snarling at each other.'

'He started it!' Grebble howled, baring her toothless gums.

'It doesn't matter,' Philomena shouted back. 'We've got bigger things to worry about.'

Alonzo sighed. 'I never thought this day would actually come – although I suppose we knew it had to.'

'W-what do you mean?' asked Bertie.

'A dusty old place like the Hippodrome wasn't going

to be around for ever, darlin',' Philomena explained. 'What was it my ma used to say? Umm . . . all good things must come to an end. I just wish it wasn't quite so sudden like.'

Ella looked up at Philomena's sad face, then down at the yellow-vested workers milling about outside. 'We can't let this happen,' she said. 'Things aren't supposed to end like this. The Ratsingers can't actually win.'

'I think they've already won, dearie,' said Madame Grebble. 'Ugh! This is giving me the morbs. Us lot can't do anything to stop 'em.'

'You could scare the workers away,' Violet said.

'Yes,' Bertie agreed. 'Ch-chase them all off!'

'Cranes and hammers can't be chased off by the likes of us,' said Grebble, shaking her head. 'We can *woo* and *boo* and rattle chains, but those thuggish machines won't care. They're all tough and rumble.'

'Well, *we* could make them stop,' Violet continued, gesturing round at Nula, Bertie and Ella.

'You?' Grebble chuckled. 'You're just lumplings and young'uns.'

'We could write a letter to the council or something.'

'That nasty little hornswoggler with the clipboard won't listen to a bunch of kiddywinks,' Grebble said. 'He wants his car park and he'll bloomin' well ignore your letters, ducky.'

191

Ella felt her stomach cartwheeling again. The old ghost was right. She looked down at the heartbreaking sight of the theatre gates lying crumpled and bent near the thicket of bushes. Those brutes had smashed their way through them with a big rusty digger. All that was left of the once-grand gateway was half a crumbling archway.

'B-but I don't w-w-want the theatre to be knocked d-down,' Bertie whimpered. He huddled in a corner and drew his knees up against his chest. 'I love it h-here.'

'Don't upset yourself so, my lad,' said Alonzo McBurnie as a tear ran down his face and dripped off his chin. 'There's no use crying at a time like this.'

'No more theatre,' Vesta mumbled.

'No more fun,' Florrie added, hugging her sister.

'No more legs!' Giuseppe bawled, making everyone jump with surprise. 'Now I'll never catch them.'

'Of course you will!' Nula exclaimed loudly, trying to sound cheerful. 'Your legs aren't going anywhere, Mr Stupendi. This'll be just like moving house, only you stay right here and a new home comes to you. I know it'll take some getting used to, but we'll weather it together.'

'That's right,' Violet agreed. 'You ghosts have resided here for years and years and, even if we can't save the theatre, I'm sure a multistorey car park won't be such a bad place to haunt. It'll be nice and breezy and we'll still

192

be able to come and visit you – and there'll be loads of other tourists to haunt . . . That'll keep you busy. It'll be a hoot!'

'Oh, my darlins',' Philomena said, her voice cracking as she started to weep. 'You don't understand.'

'What?' Nula asked, frowning. 'What don't we understand?'

'We're *theatre* ghosts,' Philomena sniffed. 'Ghosts of this theatre, and this one alone. When the Hippodrome is gone . . . so are we.'

'*Splat!*' Grebble spluttered. '*Poof! Kapow!* We'll be gone for good. Scattered to the edges of oblivion. Ta-ta for ever! See you next NEVER!'

The ancient ghost's words seemed to echo around the cramped room, prickling skin and shortening breath.

'I d-don't feel very well,' Bertie blubbed after what seemed like an eternity of silence.

'Me neither,' said Nula, looking like she might crumple in on herself. Ella had never seen her friend like this before.

'Come here, you two,' Violet said, pulling them into a hug. 'It'll be okay. We'll think of something.' She glanced across to Ella with worried, teary eyes and smiled a smile that said she didn't believe what she was saying.

'They're not going to get away with it,' blurted Ella.

She leaped to her feet, making Wilson bark, and balled her hands into fists. 'We might be kids, but we're not hopeless. Even little people can do big things. That's what my Aunt Sylvie used to say. We're not going to let Veronica's rat-faced dad destroy the theatre!'

'You heard what Grebble said,' Nula replied. 'The council aren't going to care about us. We're just a bunch of children.'

'It's true, I'm afraid,' Philomena agreed.

'Of all the times for Grebble to be right about something,' groaned Morris.

'I know!' Ella answered. 'Maybe Ratsinger won't listen to us, but we'll get the adults to help.'

'You mean get our parents to talk to them?' Violet's face brightened.

'Not *talk* . . . we'll get them to *demand*.' Ella felt like a volcano would explode inside her at any moment. She had lost too many things already before fate had brought her to Cod's Bottom. She'd lost Aunt Sylvie. She'd lost her life in London, and the jaw-trembling grumble of traffic and the hubbub of busy people, Saturday drama club, the way her old house smelled, and chocolate-chip cookie milkshakes from Alfie's Burger Bar. Ella had lost all those things, but now she had found something better than all of them. For the first time in her life, she had a whole gaggle of exciting friends to love, both living and not-so-living, and there was no way Ella would let any of them go.

'Our parents aren't enough,' she said through gritted teeth.

'Then who do you mean?' Bertie asked. 'Who's going to d-demand?'

'THE WHOLE TOWN!' Ella roared. She threw back her head and howled like a banshee as her friends scrambled to their feet and howled along with her. 'WE'LL RALLY THE WHOLE TOWN!'

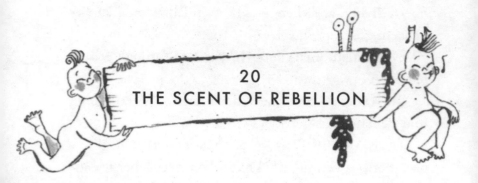

'BYE, MUM!'

The next morning couldn't have come fast enough. Ella was awake and dressed before breakfast, and she clattered out the front door with her backpack stuffed full of pens and paper, glue and glitter. She raced down Cuttlebone Lane, sweating and red-faced despite the early-morning cold, not allowing herself to stop until she reached Bertie's nan's sweet shop on Pollock Pie Alley.

'Howdy, pardner!' Violet was already outside and she greeted Ella with an American accent, tipping a pretend cowboy hat in her direction. 'You ready to fight the bad guys?'

'Ready!' Ella replied. 'It's now or never, pardner!' She picked up a pebble from the cracks in the cobbles and threw it at Bertie's bedroom window. There was a loud

CLINK, followed by a moment of quiet, before a sleepy-looking face appeared at the glass.

'Yoo-hoo! Time to save the world, Bertster! Do you always sleep through your alarm?'

Ten minutes later, the three children had made their way along the seafront to the newsagent's, where Nula was waiting on the steps.

'Morning, my merry band of outlaws,' she called. She had a folded sheet under one arm and a box of crusty paintbrushes and tins of paint under the other. Various shopping bags were littered around her feet, packed with all kinds of bright and colourful craft supplies. 'Look!' she whooped. 'Mum said we can use any old stock from the shop whenever we want! I'm so excited! I feel like Robin Hood and we're about to fight off the Sheriff of Nottingham.'

'Do you th-think we'll get into trouble?' Bertie asked, shuddering.

'Probably.' Nula nodded. 'Ratzilla will probably try to lock us in a dungeon for a thousand years.'

'We're not going to get locked in any dungeon, Bertie! Don't listen to her.' Ella smirked, rolling her eyes.

'My n-nan won't be happy if we g-get into trouble.'

'Who cares if we do?' Nula said. 'It's worth it.'

'She's right,' said Violet. 'I'll happily go to bed without dinner if it means we can save our friends.'

THE HIPPODROME IS A TREASURE

'I d-don't know,' Bertie mumbled. 'Are we b-breaking the law?'

'What do you think, Ella?' Nula turned to her and smiled. 'Will Bertie be a criminal or the hero of the Hippodrome?'

Ella glanced back at her friends and felt extremely lucky to have them. One day, when all this was over, she'd make sure to introduce them to Ava and Yusif.

'HERO OF THE HIPPODROME!' she cried.

The three girls looked at Bertie and waited for his reaction.

'I . . . um . . . er . . .' Bertie fidgeted on the spot. He frowned, until he met his friends' gaze and a smile crept into the corners of his mouth. 'L-let's go s-save the theatre!' he declared – and they were off!

'A bit more glitter over here, Pendle,' Violet called. She was standing in front of Nula's bed sheet, rubbing her chin like an artist examining her latest masterpiece. Ella and Bertie had strung up the fabric between two pillars in the foyer and now everyone was busily decorating it.

'How d-do you spell "treasure"?' Bertie asked, ducking out of the way as Pendle whizzed over his head with a pot of glue and several glitter shakers. 'I get a b-bit muddled.'

'T-R-E-S-S-H-O-O-R-E!!' Clementine Cramps spelled the word out loud with a delighted look on her face.

'That's not quite right, Clem,' Ella said, trying not to giggle.

'I think you'll find it is,' Clementine snapped back. 'I'm very good at S-P-E-L-Y-N-G, I'll have you know. I got a certificate from the workhouse once!'

Ella smiled and nodded at the bearded ghost, then leaned close to Bertie and whispered the correct spelling to him when Clementine wasn't listening.

'This all looks t'riffic,' Philomena cooed as she stood back to admire the group's handiwork. 'It looks proper smart.'

'I think it's beautiful,' said Alonzo with a sigh. 'I can knit some quick bows for the corners if you like? A few frills, no?'

'Nearly done!' Nula cheered. She and Ella had spent the last few hours making piles and piles of paper flyers with the words SAVE THE THEATRE! on them in rainbow colours, while Bertie and Violet were painting THE HIPPODROME IS A TREASURE! on the bed sheet with lots of sparkly stars and moons around it.

'Councillor Ratsinger is going to poo his pants when he sees this.' Violet laughed. 'There's no way the town can ignore us. It's Saturday – they'll all be out and about doing their shopping today. Everyone will see our posters and banner and will join in the battle.'

'We'll muster our own army and the workers won't get past the gates . . . or what's left of them.' Ella beamed. She felt incredibly proud and couldn't help thinking about the likes of Emmeline Pankhurst, or Jane Austen, or Rosa Parks or even Boudicca! Fabulous rebel women she'd read about in books, who'd stood up against all odds to achieve great things. 'I know we can do it!'

'We can!' Vesta hooted as she swung across the atrium.

'We will!' Florrie joined in. The twins somersaulted through the air and landed on either side of Ella, grinning from ear to ear.

'We believe in you,' they said. 'So do the pigeons and the woodworms.'

'The cobwebs told us,' Vesta said, nodding reassuringly.

'Twice!' Florrie added. 'They've been talking about you all morning. The saviours of the Hippodrome!'

'Who would have guessed?' Morris mused to himself from the bottom of the staircase. He glided over to Ella, tried to ruffle her hair with his icy hand, looked embarrassed when he stuck a finger through her forehead, then gave up. 'All this time you wanted to play Juliet onstage, when there's far more Hermia about you – or maybe even a spot of Rosalind.'

Ella smiled. She wasn't sure which of Shakespeare's plays Hermia or Rosalind were from, but she wrote their names in her trusty notebook and promised herself she'd look them up later.

'Yes! There's a definite whiff of hero about you, young lady,' Morris said. 'A glimmer of bravery.'

Ella felt herself secretly revelling in the idea that she might just be a rebellious hero.

'Oh, isn't that enthuzimuzzy!' Madame Grebble yawned as she floated up through the floor with Lakshmi purring on her shoulder. She doddered over to the painted sheet and regarded it thoughtfully, her gnarled hands folded across her tummy. 'I sense this might just do the trick.'

'Let us know if it doesn't . . .' Clementine mumbled absent-mindedly.

'Eh?' Nula dropped her paintbrush in a bucket of seawater and scowled at the bearded woman.

'I said, let us know if you fail.' Clementine nodded

like she didn't have a care in the world. 'I want to be wearing my best ballgown if we're all being obliterated.'

'Okay,' Nula grunted, sarcastically smiling. 'Thanks for the encouragement, Clem.'

'It's the least I can do,' Clementine sang, before drifting over to her own poster on the wall and marvelling at it.

'Ignore her. Go and show the Ratsingers you mean business,' Philomena said to the children. She tried to smile cheerfully, but her glistening eyes were filled with fear. 'Please . . . please save us . . .'

Ella held up her hand and ran her fingers through Philomena's palm.

'I promise we'll save the theatre,' she said, and prayed she wouldn't be proved wrong.

By the time eleven o'clock arrived, Ella and her friends were outside at the broken archway, ready to turn away the demolition workers.

Violet and Morris had searched about and found a pair of old mop handles under the stage, and Nula had attached them to either side of the bed sheet with string and sticky tape.

'It looks b-brilliant,' Bertie chuckled as Violet and Ella stretched the sparkly sign right across the space between the two smashed angels where the gates used to be. 'This has to d-do the t-trick.'

'We'll find out soon,' said Nula, who was armed with a stack of colourful flyers. 'Pendle? Are you there?'

Pendle replied by gently tapping all four children on the nose at once, making them squeal with surprise.

'You're such a champion!' Ella said to the poltergeist. 'A superhero!'

'The Pendle-tron 5000!' Nula declared.

'The ghost with the most!' Ella joined in. It must have been extremely uncomfortable for Pendle to venture this far away from the theatre, right on the limit of his haunt, and it made Ella tingle with admiration for her brilliantly strange friend.

'This is going to be fun,' Nula said. 'Bring it on!'

21
WE'LL FIGHT FOR OUR FRIENDS

The yellow-vested demolition workers arrived just before twelve o'clock, shuffling sleepily towards the theatre from the fishermen's yard, and by twelve thirty a crowd had gathered further down the promenade. Inquisitive shoppers and curious Cod's Bottomers wandered along the harbour wall, taking photographs and calling friends, eager to find out what all the fuss was about.

'Boss, there are kids 'ere and they won't let us through. We keep trying!' a worker in a hard hat groaned into her walkie-talkie. 'It's bonkers! I think they're protesting.'

'Nonsense!' Ella heard Councillor Ratsinger's voice crackle at the other end of the line. 'Shoo them away, for goodness' sake.'

'We really have tried,' the woman complained. 'But we can't move 'em!' For about the twentieth time, she attempted to barge the painted bed sheet out of the way, but found something was stopping her just as her body touched it.

'I don't understand,' she huffed. 'They're just really strong kiddies or something.'

'Push them away,' Councillor Ratsinger ordered. 'Fool!'

'I can't, boss! Believe me!'

'Ugh! My day is ruined! Hold on, I'll be there soon.' Ratsinger snapped before the line clicked and went dead.

Ella fizzed with glee.

'You're amazing, Pendle,' she whispered, watching the workers fussing about, trying and failing to elbow past them. Their plan was working perfectly.

Pendle patted Ella on her shoulder. The invisible ghost was doing a great job of holding the confused workers back.

'MOVE IT!' A gruff man with a round head like uncooked burger meat hollered in Nula's face. The brute reached out and tried to brush her aside, but she didn't budge an inch.

'You're going to have to do better than that,' Nula mocked, 'weakling!'

'GET OUT MY WAY!' he bellowed, seething with anger that a little girl was proving stronger than him.

'SAVE THE THEATRE!' Nula roared back even louder, then laughed as something invisible knocked the man's hard hat off and flung it into the sea like a frisbee.

'How'd you do that?' he gasped, flapping his loose jowls from side to side in astonishment.

'Must be the wind,' Nula said with a grin, then wriggled her fingers at him like she was casting a spell. 'OR WAS IT MY POWERS?' She cackled maniacally and the startled workman backed away fast.

'They don't pay me enough for this,' he grumbled.

Ella watched all this taking place and practically overflowed with joy. She felt like one of the three hundred Spartans that her old class had been reading about in a book of Greek legends last term, holding back the might of the Persian army.

'Help the Hippodrome!' she yelled, passing flyers to everyone who'd come to have a look. 'Help the Hippodrome!'

By now, more and more people from the town were wandering over to see what all the commotion was about.

'What's going on?' they asked.

'Ooh, come and look at this, Beverly.'

'They say the theatre's being pulled down to make way for a car park!'

'They can't demolish the Hippodrome!'

'Ere,' what's occurin'?'

The message was spreading across Cod's Bottom and

locals were coming out of their houses and the nearby shops in droves. Some of them grabbed flyers from Ella and stood with her, waving and yelling, and Nula's mum brought plastic cups and two enormous flasks of hot tea to pass round.

'That's my daughter, trying to save the theatre!' Mrs Wilkes beamed and told anyone who'd listen, pointing proudly at Nula. 'She's going places, she is.'

'Save the treasure of Cod's Bottom!' cried Violet.

'We m-must protect the H-Hippodrome!' Bertie shouted through a cone he'd made from a scrap of discarded cardboard. He marched back and forth in front of the banner like a guard at Buckingham Palace. 'Help the H-Hippodrome!'

Just after two o'clock, Mrs Markham from the wool shop came hurrying along the seafront with armfuls of bunting and quickly strung it up around the broken archway. The colourful little flags fluttered noisily above them in the wind, attracting even more attention.

'I came as soon as I heard what you young'uns were doing.' She smiled with kind eyes. 'You're marvellous! I've always loved the Hippodrome, sitting here like an old friend. That bully from the council can't tear it down – it's too precious.'

'Thank you, Mrs Markham,' Ella said. 'You're welcome to stay and take a stand with us, if you'd like.'

Mrs Markham needed no further encouragement. 'Right you are, dear.' She rolled up her cardigan sleeves and promptly joined in with the yelling, and she wasn't alone . . .

By three o'clock, the Johnston family, who ran the Crab and Conch Shell pub, and Mr Finch from the Laughing Starfish Store had joined the assembly and were waving flyers and chanting 'DOWN WITH CAR PARKS! DOWN WITH CAR PARKS!' Then Mr and Mrs Ghurai closed the fish shop early and brought a box of pink-and-yellow streamers left over from last year's Diwali with them, and the man who sold knick-knacks to bedraggled tourists on the pier arrived with a backpack stuffed full of silver balloons and a canister of gas to inflate them.

It didn't take long before it looked like a shimmering rainbow-coloured sea creature had appeared in front of the wrecked theatre gates. Even from the opposite end of Cod's Bottom seafront, people could spot the mass of flailing arms and multi-coloured streamer-tentacles waving in the breeze.

'Help the Hippodrome!' Ella was certain they'd be able to stop Ratsinger from building his car park with this many people supporting the fight; not to mention Pendle holding all the workers back. How could the council ignore them now? She was even more certain

of their success when, twenty minutes later, a man from the local radio station, Haddock Norton FM, arrived to ask questions. He was soon followed by a woman from the *Cod's Bottom Gazette* and two cameramen from a news channel on the television.

'We're g-going to be famous!' Bertie whispered to Ella, fidgeting with excitement.

Ella winked back at him. 'Yes. They *have* to listen to us now—'

'MOVE, YOU OAFS!!'

The voice bellowed so loudly it silenced the crowd. Everyone turned to see Councillor Ratsinger storming along the promenade towards them, with Veronica skipping behind him like an over-pampered lapdog.

'WHAT IS THE MEANING OF THIS?'

'Oh, boss, there you are!' The woman with the walkie-talkie jogged into view. 'You were ages.'

'Yes, er, I've been pony-riding,' Ratsinger spluttered, looking slightly embarrassed. 'Veronica insisted. Now, what on earth is happening? Why haven't you sent this ridiculous rabble away?'

Ella stared at the fuming man and felt the embers in her belly starting to glow again. The bonfire was back . . .

'Who are you calling "oafs" and "rabble"? Have you looked in the mirror lately?' The words flew out from between Ella's lips before she could even think about stopping herself. She clamped her hands over her mouth, but it was too late. Councillor Ratsinger froze and gawped at her, while his daughter flared her piggy nose and huffed.

'Ugh! You wish you looked like us, BUG-BURGER!' Veronica shrieked. 'Shut her up, Daddy!'

'Who exactly do you think you are, child?' Ratzilla spat the words at Ella between snarling teeth.

'She's Ella Griffin!' Violet yelled as she clambered to the top of the remaining stone gatepost. 'She's one of us, and we're all here to stop you and your RUBBISH car park!'

The crowd cheered and punched the air.

'They're weirdos, Daddy!' Veronica whinged. 'All of them!'

Councillor Ratsinger raised an eyebrow and smirked at the protesters.

'How sweet – but how incredibly stupid. You've come out today because you think streamers and a painted bed sheet are going to stop the construction of my grand car park?'

'Bog off!' Nula yelled, crouching out of sight in the crowd and giggling. 'Don't your ponies need preening?'

'Who said that?'

'Ugh! Did you brush your teeth this morning, Ratsinger?' Nula hooted even louder, imitating an old

211

man's voice. 'I can smell your breath from here. It's a rat-STINGER!'

Ratsinger grimaced with disgust as he searched for the owner of the voice. 'The fun is over,' he said, clearly failing to keep his temper. 'All of you go back to your little homes or I'll be forced to call the police. This is a demolition site and you're trespassing.'

'No!' Ella found her courage and stepped forward. *Think of Aunt Sylvie . . . Think of Aunt Sylvie . . . Think of Aunt Sylvie . . .* 'The Hippodrome has been here for over two hundred years! It should be saved, not pulled down. You can't replace a beautiful treasure with a great big ugly car park.'

'Nonsense, child!' Ratsinger grunted. 'What do you know about it? That theatre is an eyesore! A pimple! A smear of filth on our town!'

'It's a work of art!' Mrs Markham piped up.

'Imagine how gorgeous the Hippodrome could be if it was restored,' said Mrs Wilkes. 'I've loved that old place since I was a girl.'

'Me too!' Mr Johnston from the Crab and Conch Shell agreed. 'My grandma used to work in the cloakroom before it got bombed in the war.'

'WE DON'T CARE!' Veronica barked. 'GET RID OF THEM, DADDY!'

The councillor raised a hand and his vile daughter fell

silent. 'I'm sorry to disappoint you all,' he said, 'but it doesn't matter if you "love" the theatre, or if your granny worked there, or if you're the ringleader of a dreadful little rabble of troublemaking children. That pile of junk is coming down and Cod's Bottom is getting its dazzling new multistorey car park. Perfect for bringing in more tourists.'

'More tourists? Why would we want that?' Nula's mum asked.

'MONEY!' Ratsinger roared. His eyes glinted like those of one of the villains in Ella's comic books when they were thinking about world domination. 'Tourists bring MONEY!'

'Eeee!' Veronica clapped her hands and grinned. 'I love money!'

'Demolition will commence immediately,' the councillor said, rubbing his hands together like he was brushing off dirt.

'You'll have to get through us first,' Ella said. It was practically a growl.

'Idiotic child,' he shot back at her. 'Move!'

'No.'

'I. Said. Move!' Councillor Ratsinger was turning redder and redder by the second.

'NOOOO!' This time, the entire crowd yelled in unison and Ella saw a tiny flicker of concern in the joyless corners of Ratsinger's face.

'Keep your hands off our theatre,' Ella demanded. With the support of the town, she was feeling braver than she'd ever felt in her life. 'Or else!'

The two Ratsingers looked at her like she was a dog poo they'd just stepped in.

'Get her, Daddy!' Veronica hissed with spiteful glee. 'Squish her!'

Ratsinger smiled a crooked smile, then bent his head close to Ella's ear, speaking so quietly that only she could hear him: 'Are you going to stand in the way of gargantuan cranes and diggers, you silly little girl?'

'If I have to,' Ella said, making sure to stare the man-weasel straight in the eye.

'Then you'll be crushed like an insect,' he replied. 'I know all about you, Miss Griffin. You've been quite the topic of conversation up on the cliffs. You're a bad egg. All you Griffins are the same.'

'I can think of worse families,' Ella growled defiantly. 'Families who don't understand the loveliness of the Hippodrome.'

'Pah! Only hopeless dreamers could want to save a *theatre*.' The word almost made the councillor retch. 'Just like that aunt of yours before she . . .'

Ella felt every sinew of her body stiffen at the mention of her Aunt Sylvie.

214

'She was always causing problems. Raising money for libraries, or hungry children, or SAVING BLASTED DONKEYS!'

'Stupid donkeys!' Veronica scoffed. She sidled up next to her father's leg and hugged it. 'And stupid theatre! Can we knock it down now, Daddy?'

'You'll regret misbehaving like this, Miss Griffin,' Ratsinger said, his eyes filling again with fury. 'Children are supposed to be polite and silent.'

Ella shrugged. She didn't care even a tiny bit about what the councillor had to say, because, exactly at that moment, an invisible hand rested lightly on her shoulder and gave it a gentle squeeze. She'd forgotten about Pendle in all the excitement.

'I think it's time you both left,' Ella replied calmly to the fuming father and daughter. 'You're NOT demolishing the Hippodrome, not while we're here to protect it.'

'Wrong!' Ratsinger countered. 'You're coming with me. I'm going to march you straight back to that ramshackle house of yours, and we're going to have a little chat with your mother, you unruly hooligan.'

The councillor rushed forward with his daughter cackling close behind him. He reached out his bony hand, tried to grab Ella by the arm, and . . . and . . .

22
TROUBLE!

'How did this happen?' Mum gawped at Ella, her face illuminated by the flashing blue lights of a nearby police car. She'd rushed down to the harbour with Wilson in tow and was now clutching her phone in one trembling hand, glaring at the news report playing over and over again on repeat. 'My child is a criminal!'

'Er, not sure,' mumbled Ella, wincing as the footage looped and once again, the councillor and his rotten daughter flew through the air like they'd just been fired from a cannon.

'Oh, darling,' Mum groaned as she watched the Ratsingers splash down into the icy sea for the seventieth time on her phone screen. 'What were you thinking? How *could* you . . . ?'

From where the news cameraman had been filming, it certainly *looked* like Ella had done it. Besides, no one would ever believe her if she revealed that Veronica and her father had actually been launched over the harbour wall by an over-enthusiastic poltergeist. The police certainly wouldn't. 'It's impressive, but it's very wrong! You can't throw people into the sea!'

Ella looked around at all the locals being questioned by officers, and the gaggles of workers still waiting to get into the theatre grounds. At least all this bother meant the demolition had been delayed.

'I don't understand.' Mum took in the surrounding commotion with disbelief. 'Why did you do it, Ella? The last thing I expected when I turned on the news was to see my own daughter in some kind of skirmish. I thought you were out playing!'

'It's not my fault!' Ella said. 'Ratsinger is going to demolish the theatre, and—'

'That doesn't mean you can—'

'Mum, you're not listening! We can't let the Hippodrome get knocked down.' Ella glanced over at the councillor and Veronica, and felt like she might cry. The gruesome pair were huddled in blankets a little way off, wet and dishevelled, talking to a stern-looking police sergeant. Who knew what lies they'd be telling?

'Forget it, Ella. Why do you care so much about that filthy old place anyway?'

'I . . . well . . .' Ella's mind raced. Should she tell Mum

about her ghost friends and Giselle and Miss Jenkins? There was a chance she'd get into even more trouble if she did. 'Well . . . it means the world to us,' she finished.

'Who's "us"?'

'Us! Me and Violet and Bertie and Nula and . . . and, er, the rest . . .'

'"The rest"? Ella you're not making any sense. Are you in some kind of trouble . . . apart from all this?'

'No, Mum! I . . .' Ella's heart was pounding so fast she half expected to hear it knocking against her ribcage. For some reason, the idea of letting Mum know she'd been keeping secrets from her for weeks felt even worse than facing Ratsinger and his hordes of demolition workers. Mum would be so upset.

'Go easy on her, Mrs Griffin – Ella's a good girl.' It was Mrs Wilkes, Nula's mum. 'I've been here all day with the children. You should be very proud. They're standing up for something they believe in.'

Mum gasped. 'You saw them causing all this trouble?'

'The only trouble around here came from that pair of sour-faced toads.' Mrs Wilkes pointed to the Ratsingers standing near the parked police van.

'We can hear you!' Veronica shrieked as she miserably wrung out one of her plaits, yanking out a clump of seaweed that was tangled in it.

'Councillor Ratsinger said more horrible things

218

about Aunt Sylvie, Mum,' Ella blurted.

'WHAT!?' Mum looked horrified. 'Of course he didn't. He wouldn't!'

'Veronica s-said we're all weirdos, Mrs G-Griffin,' Bertie said, pointing at the dishevelled girl.

'The nasty little . . .' Mum scuffed her feet on the cobbles. Ella spotted it instantly and knew it's what Mum did when she was hopping mad about something. 'Why would she say that?'

'Because she's horrible!' Nula declared.

'Please help us, Mum,' Ella pleaded.

'I know I'm in trouble, but can't it wait until tomorrow? You can ground me all you like in the morning. I'll do the washing-up for a week if I have to, but please help us now.'

'What can we do, love?'

'We can stop them from destroying our theatre!' Ella replied.

'*Our* theatre? What do you mean, *our* theatre?' Mum's face dropped into a frown. She looked Ella in the eye, then Nula, then Violet. 'Have you—? GIRLS! Have you been sneaking into that dangerous place without telling anyone? That's SO reckless!' Mum turned on Bertie. 'Bertie, I'm surprised at you!'

Bertie snorted in horror when Mum looked his way.

'We can explain!' Ella said frantically.

'You kids could have been killed!'

'Mum, don't throw a strop-wobbler before you've heard the whole story.' Ella started jabbering so fast, her mind could hardly keep up. 'Yes, it's true – ever since we arrived in Cod's Bottom, I've been visiting the theatre with my friends, but—'

'No buts, Ella! You disobeyed me! How could you be so stupid?'

'Mum! It's wonderful in there! It's magical and our friends are in there too!'

Mum's face turned deathly pale.

'What friends? Who's in there? You mean to say there are more children inside?' she yelped. 'Oh no! OH NO! POLICE! Quick! There are children stuck inside the theatre. We've got to get them out!'

The grumpy-looking sergeant stopped talking to the Ratsingers and clomped over, raising a bristly eyebrow.

'What was that, madam?' he asked.

'There are children stuck inside the Hippodrome!' Mum wailed. 'My daughter says so!'

'No, Mum!' Ella was starting to get angry. 'Not kids! The theatre's haunted by loads and loads of spirits – more than you could count . . . Wonderful, exciting, friendly ghosts who used to know Aunt Sylvie. And if they tear the theatre down, they'll be lost for ever.' Ella could already feel her cheeks burning pink as all eyes were ogling in her direction. She must have looked like she was bonkers, but Ella was beyond caring. 'The ghosts are our friends! We've got to save them.'

'Oh, stop it, Ella,' Mum scoffed. 'Now you're just being silly.'

'It's the truth, Mrs Griffin!' Nula cut in. 'Everything Ella has just said is totally true.'

'We swear it!' Violet was soon at Ella's side, nodding anxiously. 'And it's up to us to save their home. Tell them, Bertie!'

Bertie opened his mouth to speak but nothing came out for fear of getting into trouble. Instead, he just nodded and smiled nervously.

'We're telling the truth,' Ella said to Mum and the police sergeant. 'We—'

The sound of engines suddenly caught Ella's attention and she turned to spot two large trucks driving along the seafront towards them. Vehicles weren't normally allowed on the promenade, especially giant lorries, and their dark shapes seemed alien and out of place as they rumbled around the arc of the seawall, heading straight for the theatre.

'I think we've got company,' Nula said. 'And it's not the welcome kind.'

23
TEA!!!

'Aha!' Councillor Ratsinger dumped his blanket on the cobbles and quickly straightened his damp jacket when he heard the trucks approaching. He shot a spiteful grin at Ella. 'The wrecking crew has arrived!'

Wrecking crew? Ella watched the rusty vehicles park and noticed they each had an enormous crane folded on the back of them. *This is bad . . .*

'What's all this, Ratsinger?' Nula asked. She seemed to have completely forgotten that she wasn't an adult.

'This, little girl,' he said, practically twitching with vicious joy, 'is the end of your ridiculous crusade.'

'You lost!' sneered Veronica.

No one argued back. The crowd waited in curious silence as the two lorry drivers parked, then clambered down from their cabs and wandered over to the fidgeting councillor.

'All right, boss?' one of them muttered.

'You're late,' Ratsinger snarled at him.

'And you're all wet!' the man joked back, before spotting the look of total fury on the councillor's face. 'Sorry, boss. We're not used to getting the cranes ready so fast. Very unusual.'

'I don't care,' hissed Ratsinger, drawing himself up as tall as he could. 'The theatre must be demolished immediately. Get a move on – I want it done tonight.'

'We'll have this sorted in a jiffy.'

The following minutes – or hours, it was difficult to tell – passed in a sickeningly sluggish blur as Ella and her friends were ushered aside by the police with the rest of the gathered locals. Mum kept talking – something about it probably being for the best – but Ella wasn't listening to anything she uttered. Her head was a whirl of terror and panic. What about her friends inside the Hippodrome? She stared, unblinkingly, as the trucks juddered back to life and drove straight past the broken arch, ripping the painted banner in two, snapping all the streamers and Mrs Markham's bunting.

'Where's Pendle?' Ella whimpered. 'Pendle should have stopped them.'

'Madame Grebble was right,' Nula said quietly in her ear as she took hold of Ella's and Violet's hands. 'It's not Pendle's fault. Ghosts can't fight back hulking

224

great machines. They're just too big.'

'It's hopeless,' Bertie sniffled. 'We've l-lost.'

Ella couldn't have replied if she'd wanted to. She had no idea how long they all stood and watched, but, before she knew it, the lorries were clamped into place outside the theatre entrance and their massive cranes were unfurled towards the sky with the noisy grinding of gears and creaking of rust. The demolition workers that Pendle had so bravely held back all day were now everywhere, and the sight of them preparing the two giant wrecking balls made Ella want to scream.

'We never said goodbye!' Nula wept.

'I didn't get to pet the dogs, or Lakshmi, or tell Clementine I love her,' sobbed Violet. 'Morris will never get to perform for his audience.'

'Philomena . . .' Ella mouthed the word as a tear dripped from the end of her nose. 'I *promised* her.'

'What was that, darling?' Mum asked.

'I PROMISED PHILOMENA!' Ella shouted. 'I CAN'T BREAK IT NOW!'

In an instant, she found herself shoving through the people around her and climbing to the top of the broken archway.

'Ella, what are you doing?' Mum cried, but Ella didn't reply because she didn't really know what the answer was. She just had to do *something*. ANYTHING!

225

'STOP!!' Ella screamed so loudly she nearly turned inside out.

Everybody, locals and demolition workers alike, jolted with surprise and spun round to stare. Even the deafening motors on the cranes ground to a halt and the drivers leaned out of their cabs to see what Ella was up to.

'YOU CAN'T DO THIS!' she yelled.

There was a long moment of not-quite-silence as the crowd gawped at Ella and Ella gawped back, arms lifted above her head like she was about to summon a powerful spell.

'Young lady, come down this instant,' the police sergeant barked from a little way off. 'Don't make me take you to the station – you're not too young for that, you know.'

'Arrest her, you fool!' Ratsinger ordered.

'What are you waiting for?' Veronica added. 'Lock her up!'

The sergeant ignored the councillor and his daughter, then raised a bristly eyebrow at Ella.

'I won't tell you again, miss. I understand you don't want to see the theatre knocked down. Neither do I to be honest . . . It's been here all my life. My great-great-great-grandmother performed here yonks and yonks ago. But rules are rules and we have to let the council do their business.'

'Your great-great-great-grandmother?!' Ella gasped. 'What's your name?'

'Well . . .' The sergeant squirmed uncomfortably, realizing everyone was staring at him. 'I'm Sergeant Grebble. I thought everyone knew that. Why?'

'OH!' Ella squealed with joy. 'GREBBLE!?'

'This is amazing!' Nula whooped and clambered up the broken gateway next to Ella.

'Not another one!' Sergeant Grebble moaned. 'Ladies, I—'

'We have to bring them outside!' Violet scaled the broken archway quicker than a startled squirrel and was soon next to Ella and Nula.

'They w-won't want to come out, but G-Grebble needs to meet G-Grebble!' Bertie shouted. He tried to climb up the archway but failed, so opted for striking a superhero pose in front of it instead.

Sergeant Grebble huffed at Ella's friends. 'Bring who outside? What are you on about . . . "Grebble needs to meet Grebble"?'

'They're our f-friends,' Bertie replied.

'Friends? Who?'

Ella's thoughts were zipping miles ahead already. It would take much too long to explain to every person here about the ghosts hiding, scared and frightened, inside the theatre. It might be quicker just to show the

spooks to everyone outside. She glanced
down at the sea of upturned faces and knew exactly
what needed to be done.

'TEA!' she hollered.

Nobody spoke a word. Nobody until . . .

'Eh?' Sergeant Grebble grunted.

'Tea? Why didn't you say so, poppet?' Nula's mum
stepped out of the throng with a stack of plastic cups
and a flask tucked under her arm.

'No, Mrs Wilkes,' Ella said, 'but thank you.' Then
she looked to the Hippodrome and yelled: 'PENDLE!
WE'RE PARCHED OUT HERE!'

'Who's Pendle, for goodness' sake?' Ratsinger
complained, stamping his foot in anger. 'Is someone
else in there? Sergeant Grebble, I demand you arrest
whomever it is!' Ratsinger turned to the theatre. 'We've
got you surrounded! Come out now!'

At first nothing happened and Ella worried that her
idea wasn't quite as good as she'd thought. But, after
another moment, the sudden
clatter of crockery could be
heard coming from the
open entrance doors.

'WE COULD ALL
MURDER A CUPPA, PENDLE!'
Ella shouted, and finally long lines of cracked
teacups rattling on their stained saucers came flying out
through every window and door of the theatre. They
whizzed in long rows and spiralled in circles, gliding
swiftly to the hands of every person standing outside.
Everyone except the Ratsingers, that is.

There was a moment of stunned silence, until . . .

'Stupendous!' gasped Mrs Wilkes.

'I don't believe it!' Sergeant Grebble exclaimed.

'Where are they coming from?'

'Is this some kind of magic trick?'

'I've never seen anything like it!'

'Well I never . . .' Mr Finch from the Laughing
Starfish Store chuckled. He carefully took hold of the
cup floating before him. 'It's real! For a second there, I
thought I was imagining things.'

The drivers of both cranes jumped out of their cabs,
just in time to have a cup of tea placed gently in their
hands, and even Mum, laughing like a toddler, took one
from the air.

'We didn't want to tell anyone before,' Ella announced over the nattering crowd. 'This was our secret and we wanted to keep it that way, but now I can see that we were wrong and it needs to be shared. The Hippodrome isn't empty! It's not a cold, rotten shell – or any of the other horrible things that Councillor Ratsinger has called it. It's home to hundreds of people, well . . . hundreds of GHOSTS! Brilliant, funny ghosts who are all inside there right now, scared of what's happening out here.'

'You don't realise it yet –' Nula stood up next to Ella on the broken archway – 'but you just met one of them. The cups of tea weren't a magic trick . . .'

'Nula's right,' said Ella. She thought of Pendle emptying the cobwebbed cupboards of all the bars and lounges in the entire theatre to get this many cups. 'Your tea was served by Pendle!'

'Yes,' Violet cooed. 'Pendle's a poltergeist who loves to serve tea!'

'Very s-salty s-seawater tea,' Bertie added.

There were one or two coughs and splutters around the gathering as people sipped what they'd been served. A rush of wind snatched up a pile of dried leaves from near the fence and whizzed them round and round and into the shapes of letters, until they'd spelled out *HELLO!* in mid-air.

'WOULD YOU LOOK AT THAT!' Mr Johnston

from the pub exclaimed. You mean to tell me it's all true? There have been rumours of ghosties in the town ever since I was a kid!'

'I never believed them,' hooted Mrs Wilkes. 'I even overheard you kids talking about ghosts, but I thought you were doing one of your plays.'

'They're real!' Ella said, 'and I know they'd love to meet you. They'll be listening to us right now.'

'*Pfft!* What utter hogswash!' Ratsinger marched into the centre of the crowd, beneath the levitating leaves. 'This is just a silly child's game. I can even see the strings! Look!'

'Liar!' Ella snapped back at the rat-faced man.

'I can't believe you simpletons all fell for flying cups of tea and a few—'

There was another whoosh of wind and the leaves were instantly dumped straight onto Ratsinger's head, sending him reeling and spluttering backwards like a human compost heap. Everyone laughed.

'Oh, I'm all spine-tickly!' Mrs Markham giggled as she looked on with glittering eyes. 'Are we actually going to meet real ghosts?'

'*Theatre* ghosts!' Violet corrected with a dramatic flourish of her arm. 'They're a special kind.'

'The best kind!' Nula beamed. 'And they'll love having an audience! They're very talented.'

With that, Ella and her friends climbed down from the broken archway and approached the open entrance doors. Despite the sun still setting, and the sky being vivid pink and orange, everything beyond the ticket office and cloakroom kiosk was inky black.

'It's all right,' Ella called into the gloom. 'Morris? Philomena? Alonzo? The whole town is here outside and they want to meet you. They want to see you perform. Are you there?'

Silence fell over the crowd. Actual, real silence, for the first time, as everyone and everything held its breath. The seagulls stopped cawing, the theatre stopped creaking, and even the breakers on the rocks below quietened down and listened.

'Where are they?' Violet said after a long pause.

'Shhh!' Nula nudged Violet in the ribs.

Nobody moved. Ella wasn't sure why, but she felt incredibly juddery knowing the ghosts were going to reveal themselves. It was like the first day she'd met them, all those weeks ago.

'Come on out,' she whispered through gritted teeth. 'Where are you? Come on . . .'

'See!' Ratsinger scoffed from somewhere behind Ella. 'This is all childish nonsense and lies—'

Suddenly, way back in the depths of the atrium, a tiny blue light sparked, making the crowd gasp and titter nervously as they stared into the darkness beyond the doors. They gawked as the glowing thing slowly flickered across the foyer, keeping low to the ground, heading for the open air.

'*Who* is it?' Mr Ghurai blubbed.

'*What* is it?' shrieked Mrs Ghurai.

There was a moment when even Ella wasn't sure what she was looking at, until the shimmering shape reached the front steps and an enormous ghost cat manifested itself. Lakshmi sauntered out into the gathering twilight, looked around calmly at the gobsmacked faces, mewed disdainfully as she plonked herself down on her furry rump, then stuck one of her back legs in the air and lazily licked her own bottom.

24
GHOSTS – AGAIN!

When Ella had pictured the big moment in her head, she hadn't quite seen it happening like this.

'Well, blow me down,' Mrs Markham mumbled as she goggled at Lakshmi taking a spot of very public me-time. 'I thought you meant people-ghosts, young Ella.'

'There are people-ghosts too!' Ella said. She tried to shoo Lakshmi away, but the cat refused to budge and nibbled at a phantom flea on her paw. Ella turned back to the doors and peered into the gloom, suddenly feeling slightly embarrassed. Where were her friends? 'Lots of people-ghosts. Honest!'

'I told you all, but you wouldn't listen, would you? The little rotters are making it all up!' Councillor Ratsinger jeered as he loomed over Ella. 'I demand we stop this claptrap and continue with the demolition. That's just a filthy moggy covered in glow-in-the-dark paint. Look at it – it's probably just a stray from the fishermen's ya—'

A sudden explosion of ectoplasm erupted in the air just above where Veronica and Ratzilla were standing, and Madame Grebble appeared in a flash, wringing her gnarled hands in anger.

'Who are you calling a filthy moggy, you hornswoggling, malmsey-nosed gib-face?' she rasped, jabbing a finger in the councillor's direction. The geriatric ghost was so furious she accidentally coughed her dentures out again, making Ratsinger scream as the glistening phantom gnashers sailed straight through his face and out the back of his head!

'Make it go away, Daddy!' Veronica squeaked. 'It's ugly!'

'It's just an old lady covered in glow-in-the-dark paint,' Ratsinger said, laughing unconvincingly. 'It's not real. She's on strings! Daddy knows these things.'

'Strings?' Madame Grebble grunted. 'How dare you! I haven't spent the best part of a century flyin' about to be insulted by the likes of you, you cheeky little dinlo!'

Ella would remember this moment for ever. She watched the colour drain from Ratzilla's face as he realised he was completely and utterly wrong.

All around the theatre grounds, people started gasping and pointing at the floating granny as she berated the cold-hearted councillor and his grisly daughter. The television crew pushed their way to the front of the crowd and started filming everything.

'What the bejingles do you think you're doing, coming into our theatre like you own the place?' Grebble croaked. Ella had never seen her so hot-headed. 'You're not too old for a smack on your rumples, you pigeon-livered little lump-grubs!'

'GAH!' was all Councillor Ratsinger managed to blurt, as Madame Grebble swooped down and showered him with a torrent of ectoplasmic gloop from her fingertips.

'Ha ha! Take that, you stinking gruzzler!' she cackled. 'Now who's a moggy?'

236

Ella couldn't stop herself from grinning. This was turning out to be so much better than she'd hoped. Not only was Ratsinger being shamed on national television, but Madame Grebble was being broadcast across the country to millions of viewers! With proof that ghosts haunted the Hippodrome, there was no way it would be destroyed now. The theatre would become the pride of Cod's Bottom and would attract far more tourists than a stupid car park!

'Children!'

Ella looked up just in time to see Philomena appear in a glittering explosion on a first-floor window ledge.

'You little wonders!' Philomena whooped as the Cod's Bottomers *ooh*ed and *aah*ed at her. 'Is it done? Are we saved?'

'It's done!' Nula called up to the dazzling ghost. 'I think!'

'Bloomin' brilliant!' Philomena cried, then she leaped from the ledge and loop-the-looped in the air, before floating down amongst the astonished crowd. She raised her fingers to her lips and let rip with an ear-jangling whistle. 'Come on, ladies – let's put on a show!'

In a heartbeat, Allegra, Electra and Olympia came bounding out through the red-and-gold doors, jumping and chasing excitedly straight through the astounded locals. And all around, the sounds of sudden bursts of

237

ectoplasm could be heard, as more of the Hippodrome's ghosts appeared. Ella turned on the spot and took in the scene with a warm feeling in her tummy.

'Greetings, friendly theatregoers!' Morris boomed in his best Shakespearian voice as he manifested at the base of one of the cranes. He swept into a low bow. 'Allow me to introduce myself: I am Octavius P. Gulch – the Toast of London, the Pride of Piccadilly, the Bard of Bermondsey, the—'

'A COW DID THAT IN GRANDMA'S HAT!' Clementine Cramps twinkled into view in full song, hitting such a shrill high note that Mr and Mrs Ghurai cowered and covered their ears. Then the ghostly band of musicians appeared, sitting along the edge of the stained-glass dome, and struck up a jazzy tune as the audience apparitions started to flicker into view, ready to watch the evening's haunted spectacular. It was as if all the human activity had set the Hippodrome dreaming, and the spectres materialised where the gates used to be, hurrying excitedly towards the theatre's entranceway. They gathered at the windows, hustling and bustling in the galleries, sipping phantom cocktails and chattering to phantom friends.

'Behold!' Alonzo McBurnie flexed his muscles on the front steps and the Tunk Twins gracefully cartwheeled over the audience's heads.

'This is tremendous,' Violet said to Ella, giving her hand a squeeze. 'You did it! The Hippodrome is saved.'

Both girls jolted with surprise as earsplitting screeching erupted behind them. They spun on their heels and hopped aside as the Ratsingers suddenly ran through the theatre grounds – with Giuseppe's disembodied legs chasing after them.

'This is most disorderly!' Ratzilla huffed as he thudded past. 'Go away!'

'AAGH! What are they, Daddy!?' Veronica wailed, sprinting towards the promenade.

'They're just . . . legs . . .' he wheezed, 'with glow-in-the-dark paint on them . . .'

'*Daddy* – I WANT TO GO HOME!'

Violet put her arms round Ella's neck and hugged her tightly. 'You're a hero,' she said, before politely pulling away. 'Oh . . . er . . . I think someone finally wants to talk to you.'

Ella glanced at Violet, then turned to see what she was looking at over her shoulder. Ghosts and living people alike fell silent as a pale blue glow, no bigger than a tiny pinprick, shone from one of the top-floor windows. It flashed and glistened in the early-evening gloom and, as if in response to it, one of the ghost violinists started playing a beautifully sad song. The tune was lilting and melancholic, and the glowing shape seemed to react as

239

his bow skimmed the phantom strings.

Ella hardly dared to breathe. She watched as the orb of light floated out through the broken glass and sparkled in the outside air, drifting softly downwards.

'If that's Lakshmi again,' Nula muttered under her breath, 'I'll scream.'

'Fingers crossed it's not,' Violet whispered.

As the violinist continued to play, the light began to twist and pulsate to the beautiful music. Delicate tendrils of smoke started to drift from its centre and, before Ella had even realised, they had changed into swiftly moving arms and legs. It was the ballerina!

The crowd heaved a collective sigh as the violin played faster and, overhead, Giselle's dance intensified. She swooped and leaped and twirled through the breeze, pirouetting masterfully, until . . .

'MOVE IT!' a voice in the crowd croaked. 'MAKE WAY!'

25
IT CAN'T END LIKE THIS

Everyone turned to see a tiny woman in a purple cake-tin hat hobbling through the crowd. Looking pale and alarmed she waved her sticks and wobbled forwards – 'Let me through, you great lumps!' – and Ella couldn't believe who it was. When had Miss Jenkins arrived?

'Evelyn!' Mum gasped, rushing over to help the old lady. 'How long have you been here?'

'Long enough!' Miss Jenkins snarled. 'You didn't think I'd miss it, when I saw all these shenanigans on the telly did you? The news channels are all going bonkers about it.'

'How did you get here?' Ella asked, approaching the grannysaurus cautiously.

'That one!' Miss Jenkins pointed a stick at a nervous-looking Mrs Clott.

'I was just cooking my dinner when Evelyn pounded

on my door and told me to help her down to the Hippodrome,' Tabitha whimpered. 'I didn't dare say no.'

'Well, it's a good thing you didn't, Clott,' Miss Jenkins snapped, 'or I would have shoved my sticks right where . . . Well, never mind – I'm here now, and I want to talk to these ghost friends of yours, Griffin girl. I think they might know my—'

Miss Jenkins' voice trailed off as she spotted the dancer twirling overhead.

'Oh, my *sister*!'

Giselle looked around like someone who'd just realised they'd been caught in a trap. She turned to fly back towards the theatre, but Miss Jenkins lurched forwards, raising her arms above her head before the ghostly-girl had even reached the windows

'Sister!' Miss Jenkins cried. All the anger had vanished from her voice. 'My Giselle!'

Giselle froze in mid-air and the window ledges near her suddenly prickled with icicles.

'Don't go, sister!' Miss Jenkins blubbed. 'It's me – your Evelyn. I'm still here, my petal. I've found you!'

The ghost didn't react at first. She floated in place until curiosity finally got the better of her and she glanced over her shoulder.

'My Giselle!' Miss Jenkins sobbed with happiness when, finally, she locked eyes with her unfamiliar twin.

Giselle suddenly shimmered with a rainbow of colours as ice crackled across the ground around everyone's feet and up over the rooftops of the theatre.

'Oh, it *is* you,' said Evelyn Jenkins. 'I thought I'd lost you for ever, my darling sister!'

The ballerina smiled.

Music filled the air as ghosts and living alike celebrated outside the theatre. The night was lit by hundreds of tiny blue wisps that hung there like candle flames. Clementine serenaded the demolition workers, the Tunk Twins played with Nula, Violet and Bertie, teaching them to cartwheel, and Alonzo sat gossiping with Mrs Markham from the wool shop.

Madame Grebble, meanwhile, sat on the ground offering psychic readings to all the police officers after discovering that her great-great-great-grandson was the Cod's Bottom sergeant.

'Oh, look at that mug,' she cooed, peering at the startled man over her spectacles. 'Bee-*yoo*-tiful!' the ancient fortune teller cackled, baring her nearly empty gums. 'We're family, all right!'

With the unexpected good news, Sergeant Grebble made an announcement to the crowd that he would be making immediate enquiries about turning the Hippodrome into a ghostly nature reserve, forbidding

any demolition and forcing the council to pay for its upkeep.

Everything was perfect.

Ella sat cross-legged on the top of the broken archway and smiled to herself. Her trusty green notebook was in her lap and she was writing down every detail. ALL OF IT! She didn't want to miss a thing as she looked round at the happy faces. Evelyn and Giselle Jenkins were chatting and crying happily on the entrance steps; Mum was giggling with Philomena over by the big barbecue that Mr Johnston had brought from the pub; and Morris . . . where was Morris?

Ella searched for the actor-ghost amongst all the revellers. Her eyes moved serenely over the cheerful scene until something out-of-place caught her attention . . .

The door to one of the crane cabins on the far side of the grounds was hanging open, and a girl with long dark plaits down her back was standing on the outside platform furiously gesturing at a man sitting in the controller's seat. The man was kicking and yanking at levers and pedals, shunting back and forth in the chair, visibly frantic.

Ella wasn't entirely sure what happened next. She vaguely remembered screaming and scrambling down from the archway, but the memory was hazy. By the time she'd reached the foot of the crane, others had noticed what was happening too and cries of alarm broke the joyful mood of the evening.

Ratzilla and Veronica must have sneaked back past the revellers and were now frenziedly trying to work the rusty machine!

'Councillor Ratsinger! Step away from the crane!' Sergeant Grebble ordered, but the revolting pair refused to even look at him. 'I mean it, sir!'

'Don't you tell me what to do, Sergeant – I KNOW WHAT'S BEST FOR YOU ALL!' Ratsinger declared. He jabbed at one of the levers and the enormous contraption juddered on its truck-base, making the wrecking ball swing out across the theatre grounds. People dived in all directions to avoid being hit, and Mr Johnston's barbecue was obliterated in an instant.

'Get them, Daddy!' Veronica sneered. 'Show them all!'

'I *will* have MY CAR PARK! And you'll thank me for it – EVERY LAST ONE OF YOU!' Councillor Ratsinger looked out over the crowd and Ella knew right then that it was hopeless. 'PARLIAMENT AWAITS! I'll be the pride of Cod's Bottom! Hold on, darling! DADDY'S GOING TO FIX EVERYTHING!'

A wide and hysterical grin stretched across Ratsinger's twitching face, and his eyes burned with determination. This wasn't the expression of a councillor who really wanted a car park. Ella knew that much. This was the look of someone who had never been told *NO*. It was the look of someone who'd been spoiled since childhood, who'd been taught that creativity was weakness, and bullying was strength, and difference was ugliness, and anyone who thought otherwise was either stupid or beneath them. It was the look of someone who could never begin to fathom that they were wrong.

'I WILL HAVE MY CAR PARK!'

The crane lurched in a circle, bringing the wrecking ball careering after it.

'Get them, Daddy!'

The sickening crunch of the iron ball exploding through the theatre's brickwork would echo around Ella's thoughts for weeks after that night as she constantly replayed it in her mind like a slow-motion, nightmarish movie.

It only took a few hits . . .

Ratsinger laughed like a demented hyena as the crane struck the Hippodrome for a second time, then a third, toppling the glass dome and most of the entrance.

Ella remembered the moment of absolute silence as the wrecking ball came to a standstill, that eerie split second before a skeleton-rattling crack resounded off the cliffs and – it was difficult to think about – the wooden stilts beneath the grand building gave way, and, like a wedding cake perched too close to the edge of the table, the Hippodrome collapsed into the cold and spiteful sea.

Horror was etched on every face. Howls of anguish filled the air.

Ella turned to Philomena just in time to catch her panic-stricken eyes, and then, like dust scattered on the wind, the ghosts of the Hippodrome were gone.

26
EVERYBODY LOVES AN AUDIENCE

Three weeks passed and the television crews finally gave up.

Every day since the Hippodrome had been demolished, journalists and ghost-hunters and radio reporters had come knocking at Minerva Mansions, eager to find out more about the incident in Cod's Bottom, but Ella and Mum refused to speak to any of them. What was there to say?

It was a Monday lunchtime and Ella stood at her bedroom window with Nula, Violet and Bertie, staring out towards where the theatre used to be at the end of the promenade.

'At least—' Bertie mumbled after what could have been hours.

'Hmmm?' Nula grunted.

'At least R-Ratsinger got what he deserved.'

'That's true.' Violet nodded. She smiled, but Ella could tell it was only a pretend smile.

'Sergeant Grebble stopped by yesterday,' Ella said. 'He thinks Ratsinger will end up in prison.' She wanted to feel happy, knowing that councillor Ratsinger had been arrested for endangering lives, but it didn't feel like a victory. Not really.

'At least Veronica will NEVER be prime minister now,' Violet half chuckled.

'But she will b-be prime –' Bertie thought for a moment – 'poo!'

For the first time in weeks, everybody laughed.

'Come on, we can't mope around like this for ever,' Nula said after a while. She walked away from the window and jumped onto the bed where Wilson was snoring. 'Let's do something fun.'

Ella shook her head. 'I'm not in the mood.'

'M-me neither,' Bertie agreed.

'But Philomena and Morris would be so mad if they knew we'd all turned into a bunch of whingers,' argued Nula.

'I like whinging!' Violet joked back. 'I'm really good at it now.'

'Well, try to think of something else,' Nula encouraged.

'I can't,' Ella said, jumping onto the bed next to her. 'Everything reminds me of them.'

'Not everything!' Nula demanded.

'EVERYTHING!' Ella replied.

Nula reached over the side of the bed and snatched up a dirty sock from one of Bertie's discarded trainers. 'Even this?' she asked.

'Ugh! It smells like mouldy cheese,' Violet said with a sad smile. 'So did the Hippodrome carpets.'

Nula leaped up and grabbed a stuffed toy from the floor.

'This?'

'It's soft and s-squishy,' said Bertie. 'It makes me miss the poodles.'

'This?' Nula pointed to the framed picture of Frida Kahlo on the wall.

'She's brilliant and beautiful,' Ella moaned. 'Just like Philomena.'

Nula looked exasperated. 'Oh, come on, whingers!' She wandered over to the bookshelves and pointed to the books and scripts. 'And these?'

'Morris would have loved those,' Violet said.

'And that's where I saw Giselle,' Ella added. 'She was standing right there.'

'No she wasn't!' Nula laughed back at Ella. 'We told you before.'

'YES SHE WAS!' Ella roared in mock-outrage. 'I promise I'm not lying. She really was RIGHT THERE.'

252

'The only thing worse than a whinger is a whinger who tells fibs,' Nula teased.

'I'm not telling fibs!' Ella clambered off the bed. 'Ugh! I wish I'd had time to ask Giselle about it – before . . .'

'I b-believe you,' said Bertie with a smile.

'Thanks, Bertster,' Ella replied glumly. 'I promise I'm not lying though. Giselle was standing right here, next to the little hand on the shelf.'

'Eh?' Nula grunted again.

'The hand! . . . I forgot about it—' Ella searched the shelves but they were empty. 'Where is that thing?'

'What are you talking about?' Violet asked.

Ella didn't answer. She was looking around her bedroom, trying to sort through the memories of her mad time in Cod's Bottom. What had she done with the little stone hand she'd found on her first trip to the theatre?

'It was here,' she mumbled.

'Hello? EARTH TO ELLA!' said Nula in her best robot voice.

'Ella?' Violet said a little louder.

'ELLA!' Bertie yelled, louder still.

Ella looked up and realised her friends were all staring at her.

'Sorry,' she said. 'I was miles away.'

'What are you mumbling about?' Nula asked. 'Don't go loopy on us now.'

'I just remembered, I had a . . .' Ella walked over to where her coat hung on the back of her bedroom door. She plunged her hand into the pockets and rummaged around.

The right pocket . . . nothing.

The left pocket . . . nothing.

'It must be here *some*where,' Ella said.

'WHAT?' Nula barked. 'You're not making any sense!'

Ella unzipped the little inside pocket where she always kept a spare pen for list-making emergencies. She felt inside and her fingers grazed against something cold and hard.

'Aha!' Ella whooped, producing the tiny cherub's hand. 'This! I'd completely forgotten about it.'

'W-what is it?' Bertie asked.

Ella passed it over and watched her friends take turns examining the little object.

'I found it outside the theatre gates,' she explained, 'and haven't thought about it in ages.'

'Well, whoever it belonged to,' Violet said, 'I don't think they'll be needing it now.'

'Aw,' Bertie sighed. 'A little p-piece of the Hippodrome.'

Ella nodded. 'It was on the shelf just there, the night Giselle appeared,' she said.

'Hang on . . .' Nula turned to Ella. 'You're saying you had this here in your room?'

'Yes.' Ella nodded again. 'Why?'

'This changes everything!'

'What do you mean?' Violet asked.

'You didn't tell us about the hand, even though it's MASSIVELY important!' Nula cried, smacking her forehead.

'I don't understand,' Ella replied.

'It's impossible for ghosts to leave their haunts, right?' Nula jumped up and turned to everyone like she was teaching a class.

'R-right,' agreed Bertie.

'So Giselle couldn't come to your house—'

'But she did!' Ella groaned. This was getting exhausting!

'No, listen a minute,' Nula said, 'I'm just working it out.' She looked down at the stone hand and her eyes widened. 'Giselle was here because THIS PIECE OF THE THEATRE WAS HERE. You saw her in your room – but she was still haunting THE HIPPODROME.'

'So?' Bertie looked like he was about to topple off the bed.

'So our friends' haunt hasn't completely gone!' Nula hooted. 'We've got a piece of it right here!'

Nula placed the tiny hand in the centre of the bed and everyone huddled round. They all stared at it for a very long time . . .

'Is something supposed to happen?' Violet mumbled.

'*Hmm*, not sure,' Nula said. She looked at Ella and frowned. 'Take us through everything.'

'Huh?'

'Tell us everything you did that night.'

'Did you cast any spells on it?' Violet asked with a giggle.

'Did you r-rub it like a magic l-lamp?' Bertie joined in.

'Um, no.' Ella tried to think back to that stormy night. 'We'd got drenched in the rain,' she said. 'When we got back in, I came upstairs and took off my coat and wellies . . .'

'I d-don't think that bit matters,' said Bertie.

'. . . I'd found the hand by the theatre – before I saw Giselle in one of the top-floor windows. I'd brought it home, put it on my shelf,' Ella went on, 'and I was thinking about Giselle and I talked to the hand.'

'Ha!' Nula snorted.

'No, not like that,' Ella laughed. 'I always talk to things.'

'That's it!' Violet said. 'Don't you see? They're theatre ghosts – and you gave this little bit of the Hippodrome some attention.'

'Everyone loves an audience . . .' Ella muttered under her breath.

'That's what must have invited Giselle into your room!' Nula said. 'She must have wanted a way of getting closer to her sister, and you gave it to her.'

The four children stared at the stone hand.

'Say something, Ella,' Violet instructed.

'I don't know what to say.'

There was another long pause before Bertie carefully picked it up.

'I'll do it,' he said with a confident smile. 'I'm b-best at this.' Bertie took a deep breath and shouted: 'THERE ARE FOUR CHILDREN HERE WHO W-WANT THEIR FRIENDS BACK. THEY'RE BORED AND N-N-NEED TO BE ENTERTAINED!'

Everybody held their breath.

Nothing . . .

Nothing . . .

Ella sighed to herself. It was silly to have hoped, even for a second. She opened her mouth to speak and—

SPLOOF! The unmistakable sound of ectoplasm exploding behind them made everyone jolt with surprise and the hairs on the back of their necks stand on end.

SPLAT!

WHOOSH!

SPLOOSH!

PLISH!

Ella could feel her friends trembling. They all remained hunched over the little hand and no one dared to turn round and look . . . not until an enormous glowing cat jumped up onto the bed, peered moodily at the four children and the snoring dog, then plonked herself down on her fluffy rump and lazily licked her bottom.

Ella sat alone in her room and smiled to herself.

Six months had passed since the Hippodrome Ghosts had re-materialised and Minerva Mansions was officially renamed High Spirits House: Rest Home For the Not-so-living.

The ghosts had happily moved into their new haunt and even the humans didn't mind having them around.

Philomena and her poodles spend most of their time in the kitchen nowadays, where they entertain Mum while she cooks dinner. Morris and Clementine give nightly performances in the living room, Madame Grebble stalks the staircases, Alonzo nabbed himself the nice safe toilet to call his own, the Tunk Twins spend most of their time somersaulting on the roof amongst the chimneypots and Giuseppe Stupendi still hasn't caught his legs, but he's pretty certain he saw them going into Mrs Clott's apartment.

It was the happy ending Ella had hoped for.

Miss Jenkins can usually be found out in the hallway these days, practising ballet with Giselle as she grips the banister and moans about her creaking joints, and Pendle helps out, making REAL cups of tea for anyone who'll drink them.

'Perfect,' Ella said to nobody in particular, then sat down at her desk and pulled out the notebook Nula had given her from the newsagent's.

She hadn't been able to write a list since the night of the demolition. Her head had been too full of whooshy thoughts and jumbled emotions to concentrate. But the sight of fresh blank paper had ignited an extra-special idea for what Ella wanted to include in her brand-new notebook. 'This requires something grander than a list,' she told Wilson.

Picking up her trusty green pen, she turned to the first page and scribbled . . .

Spooked –
The Theatre Ghosts

Then Ella thought of Aunt Sylvie, took one last glance at the stone hand sitting on her bookshelf, and started to write.

ACKNOWLEDGEMENTS

Armfuls of gratitude to the Society of Authors whose Work in Progress grant afforded me the time and funds to tippy-type away without any writer's angst, stress and worry.

A huge hug of appreciation to Jane Griffiths, Amina Youssef and Lowri Ribbons: the three brilliant ladies who commissioned, edited and tweaked *Spooked: The Theatre Ghosts* into the book it is today.

Claire Powell realised Ella and her merry band of misfits with a witty eye and hilarious talent. I don't believe anyone could have made the book look lovelier. Thank you! Thank you! THANK YOU!

Lots of love to Francesca Simon for listening to me bounce a thousand ideas around, Steven Lenton for keeping me sane and all you HONKHUMPTIOUS readers out there! Without booky kids like you, us writers would have no one to make books for.

STEVEN BUTLER is an award-winning and *New York Times* bestselling author, performer and voice artist. His books have won the coveted Sainsbury's Children's Book Award, and been shortlisted for the Roald Dahl Funny Prize, Alligator's Mouth Award and the Lollies. Having spent most of his adult life performing in London's West End and around the UK, Steven has been collecting spooky tales and superstitious rumours about haunted theatres for years and years and knew it was time to write about his own gaggle of ghosties.

When he isn't writing books, Steven can often be found obsessing about spices and home cooking in his tiny London kitchen, or spending time in Brighton with his pet dog, Big-Eared Bob.

CLAIRE POWELL is a bestselling children's book illustrator who initially started out designing for big-hitting television brands, before an impromptu visit to a children's book exhibition led her down the path of illustration. Self-taught, Claire got her first book deal in 2015 and has never looked back.

A hugely versatile artist, Claire has a talent for creating characters that are brimming with emotion and personality, her sense of humour often infuses her work, which has topped the charts on several occasions. After spending many years in London, Claire now enjoys a quieter life in the rolling hills of Derbyshire with her partner, Stefan . . . who may not agree that living with Claire is quiet.

Have you checked out

Frankie Banister's

blunkingly bonkers adventures in

The Nothing to See Here Hotel series?